"A BANQUET OF RICHES . . .

Wickedly funny yet haunting and melancholy . . . Adams astonishes us by her ability to create within a few pages an event, or relationship, or life of such depth and richness that we become instantly and permanently fastened to it."
—*San Francisco Examiner & Chronicle*

"Alice Adams speaks to me. She writes about lives you believe in. She knows so much about how intelligent people feel and think . . . superb writing."
—*The Boston Globe*

"Alice Adams turns dreams and moments, the stuff of memories, inside out and makes of them beautiful, haunting bittersweet tales."
—*Publishers Weekly*

"Alice Adams at her best, writing vividly about characters we care for."
—*Chicago Tribune Book World*

"She belongs with the best contemporary writers of short fiction . . . artistic near-perfection."
—*Kansas City Star*

ALICE ADAMS is the author of four novels, *Careless Love, Families and Survivors, Listening to Billie* and *Rich Rewards.* Her short stories have appeared regularly in numerous magazines including *The New Yorker, Atlantic Monthly* and *Redbook,* and have been represented in every O. Henry Award collection for the past nine years. She has been the recipient of grants from the Guggenheim Foundation and the National Foundation for the Arts. She lives in San Francisco.

Beautiful Girl

Stories by

ALICE ADAMS

WASHINGTON SQUARE PRESS
PUBLISHED BY POCKET BOOKS NEW YORK

All stories in this book except for "A Pale and Perfectly Oval Moon," "Attrition" and "What Should I Have Done?" have previously been published in *The Atlantic Monthly, Charm, Mademoiselle, The New Yorker, Paris Review, Redbook* and *The Virginia Quarterly Review.*

Grateful acknowledgment is made to the following to reprint previously published material:

Big Sky Music: For use of lyrics from "Lay, Lady, Lay" by Bob Dylan. Copyright © 1969 by Big Sky Music. Used by permission. All Rights Reserved.

Warner Bros., Inc.: For use of lyrics from "It Ain't Me, Babe" by Bob Dylan. Copyright © 1964 by Warner Bros., Inc. Used by permission. All rights reserved.

Mills Music, Inc.: For use of lyrics from "When It's Sleepy Time Down South" by Leon Otis, Rene Otis and Clarence Muse. Copyright 1931 by Mills Music, Inc. Copyright renewed. Used with permission. All rights reserved.

 WSP A Washington Square Press Publication of
POCKET BOOKS, a Simon & Schuster division of
GULF & WESTERN CORPORATION
1230 Avenue of the Americas, New York, N.Y. 10020

Published by arrangement with Alfred A. Knopf, Inc.
Library of Congress Catalog Card Number: 78-54932

ISBN: 0-671-83218-2

First Washington Square Press printing March, 1981

10 9 8 7 6 5 4 3 2 1

WASHINGTON SQUARE PRESS, WSP and colophon are trademarks of Simon & Schuster.

Printed in the U.S.A.

For
William Abrahams
and Peter Stansky

Contents

THE TODDS

Verlie I Say Unto You

Every morning of all the years of the Thirties, at around seven, Verlie Jones begins her long and laborious walk to the Todds' house, two miles uphill. She works for the Todds—their maid. Her own house, where she lives with her four children, is a slatted floorless cabin, in a grove of enormous sheltering oaks. It is just down a gravelly road from the bending highway, and that steep small road is the first thing she has to climb, starting out early in the morning. Arrived at the highway she stops and sighs, and looks around and then starts out. Walking steadily but not in any hurry, beside the winding white concrete.

First there are fields of broomstraw on either side of the road, stretching back to the woods, thick, clustered dark pines and cedars, trees whose lower limbs are cluttered with underbrush. Then the land gradually rises until on one side there is a steep red clay bank, going up to the woods; on the other side a wide cornfield, rich furrows dotted over in spring with tiny wild flowers, all colors—in the winter dry and rutted, sometimes frosted over, frost as shiny as splintered glass.

Then the creek. Before she comes to the small

9

concrete bridge, she can see the heavier growth at the edge of the fields, green, edging the water. On the creek's steep banks, below the bridge, are huge peeling poplars, ghostly, old. She stands there looking down at the water (the bridge is halfway to the Todds'). The water is thick and swollen, rushing, full of twigs and leaf trash and swirling logs in the spring. Trickling and almost dried out when summer is over, in the early fall.

Past the bridge is the filling station, where they sell loaves of bread and cookies and soap, along with the gas and things for cars. Always there are men sitting around at the station, white men in overalls, dusty and dried out. Sometimes they nod to Verlie. "Morning, Verlie. Going to be any hot day?"

Occasionally, maybe a couple of times a year, a chain gang will be along there, working on the road. The colored men chained together, in their dirty, wide-striped uniforms, working with their picks. And the thin, mean guard (a white man) with his rifle, watching them. Looking quickly, briefly at Verlie as she passes. She looks everywhere but there, as her heart falls down to her stomach and turns upside down. All kinds of fears grab at her, all together: she is afraid of the guard and of those men (their heavy eyes) and also a chain gang is one of the places where her deserting husband, Horace, might well be, and she never wants to see Horace again. Not anywhere.

After the filling station some houses start. Small box houses, sitting up high on brick stilts. On the other side of the highway red clay roads lead back into the hills, to the woods. To the fields of country with no roads at all, where sometimes Mr. Todd goes to hunt rabbits, and where at other times, in summer, the children, Avery and Devlin Todd, take lunches and stay all day.

From a certain bend in the highway Verlie can see the Todds' house, but she rarely bothers to look anymore. She sighs and shifts her weight before starting up the steep, white, graveled road, and then the road to the right that swings around to the back of the house, to the back door that leads into the kitchen.

There on the back porch she has her own small bathroom that Mr. Todd put in for her. There is a mirror and some nails to hang her things on, and a flush toilet, ordered from Montgomery Ward, that still works. No washbasin, but she can wash her hands in the kitchen sink.

She hangs up her cardigan sweater in her bathroom and takes an apron off a nail. She goes into the kitchen to start everyone's breakfast.

They all eat separate. First Avery, who likes oatmeal and then soft-boiled eggs; then Mr. Todd (oatmeal and scrambled eggs and bacon and coffee); Devlin (toast and peanut butter and jam); and Mrs. Todd (tea and toast).

Verlie sighs, and puts the water on.

❦

Verlie has always been with the Todds; that is how they put it to their friends. "Verlie has always been with us." Of course, that is not true. Actually she came to them about ten years before, when Avery was a baby. What they meant was that they did not know much about her life before them, and also (a more important meaning) they cannot imagine their life without her. They say, "We couldn't get along without Verlie," but it is unlikely that any of them (except possibly Jessica, with her mournful, exacerbated and extreme intelligence) realizes the full truth of the remark. And, laughingly, one of them will add, "No one else could put up with us." Another truth, or perhaps only a partial truth: in those days, there and then, most maids put up with a lot, and possibly Verlie suffers no more than most.

She does get more money than most maids, thirteen dollars a week (most get along on ten or eleven). And she gets to go home before dinner, around six (she first leaves the meal all fixed for them), since they—since Mr. Todd likes to have a lot of drinks and then eat late.

Every third Sunday she gets off to go to church.

None of them is stupid enough to say that she is like a member of the family.

❧⳺❧

Tom Todd, the handsome, guiltily faithless husband, troubled professor (the 10 percent salary cuts of the Depression; his history of abandoned projects—the book on Shelley, the innumerable articles)—Tom was the one who asked Verlie about her name.

"You know, it's like in the Bible. Verlie I say unto you."

Tom felt that he successfully concealed his amusement at that, and later it makes a marvelous story, especially in academic circles, in those days when funny-maid stories are standard social fare. In fact people (white people) are somewhat competitive as to who has heard or known the most comical colored person, comical meaning outrageously childishly ignorant. Tom's story always goes over well.

❧⳺❧

In her summer sneakers, shorts and little shirt, Avery comes into the dining room, a small, dark-haired girl carrying a big book. Since she has learned to read (her mother taught her, when she was no bigger than a minute) she reads all the time, curled up in big chairs in the living room or in her own room, in the bed. At the breakfast table.

"Good morning, Verlie."

"Morning. How you?"

"Fine, thank you. Going to be hot today?"

"Well, I reckon so."

Avery drinks her orange juice, and then Verlie takes out the glass and brings in her bowl of hot oatmeal. Avery reads the thick book while she eats. Verlie takes out the oatmeal bowl and brings in the soft-boiled eggs and a glass of milk.

"You drink your milk, now, hear?"

Verlie is about four times the size of Avery and more times than that her age. (But Verlie can't read.)

Verlie is an exceptionally handsome woman, big and tall and strong, with big bright eyes and smooth yellow skin over high cheekbones. A wide curving mouth, and strong white teeth.

Once there was a bad time between Avery and Verlie: Avery was playing with some children down the road, and it got to be suppertime. Jessica sent Verlie down to get Avery, who didn't want to come home. "Blah blah blah blah!" she yelled at Verlie—who, unaccountably, turned and walked away.

The next person Avery saw was furious Jessica, arms akimbo. "How are you, how *could* you? Verlie, who's loved you all your life? How could you be so cruel, calling her black?"

"I didn't—I said blah. I never said black. Where is she?"

"Gone home. Very hurt."

Jessica remained stiff and unforgiving (she had problems of her own); but the next morning Avery ran down into the kitchen at the first sound of Verlie. "Verlie, I said blah blah—I didn't say black."

And Verlie smiled, and it was all over. For good.

Tom Todd comes into the dining room, carrying the newspaper. "Good morning, Avery. Morning, Verlie. Well, it doesn't look like a day for getting out our umbrellas, does it now?"

That is the way he talks.

"Avery, please put your book away. Who knows, we might have an absolutely fascinating conversation."

She gives him a small sad smile and closes her book. "Pass the cream?"

"With the greatest of pleasure."

"Thanks."

But despite the intense and often painful complications of his character, Tom's relationship with Verlie is perhaps the simplest in that family. Within their rigidly defined roles they are even fond of each other. Verlie thinks he talks funny, but not much more so than most men—white men. He runs around with women (she knows that from his handkerchiefs, the lipstick stains that he couldn't have bothered to hide from her) but not as much as Horace did. He bosses his wife and children but he doesn't hit them. He acts as Verlie expects a man to act, and perhaps a little better.

And from Tom's point of view Verlie behaves like a Negro maid. She is somewhat lazy; she does as little cleaning as she can. She laughs at his jokes. She sometimes sneaks drinks from his liquor closet. He does not, of course, think of Verlie as a woman—a woman in the sense of sexual possibility; in fact he once sincerely (astoundingly) remarked that he could not imagine a sexual impulse toward a colored person.

❦

Devlin comes in next. A small and frightened boy, afraid of Verlie. Once as he stood up in his bath she touched his tiny penis and laughed and said, "This here's going to grow to something nice and big." He was terrified: what would he do with something big, down there?

He mutters good morning to his father and sister and to Verlie.

❧❦❧

Then Jessica. Mrs. Todd. "Good morning, everyone. Morning, Verlie. My, doesn't it look like a lovely spring day?"

She sighs, as no one answers.

❧❦❧

The end of breakfast. Verlie clears the table, washes up, as those four people separate.

❧❦❧

There is a Negro man who also (sometimes) works for the Todds, named Clifton. Yard work: raking leaves in the fall, building a fence around the garbage cans, and then a dog kennel, then a playhouse for the children.

When Verlie saw Clifton the first time he came into the yard (a man who had walked a long way, looking for work), what she thought was: Lord, I never saw no man so beautiful. Her second thought was: He sick.

Clifton is bronze-colored. Reddish. Shining. Not brown like most colored (or yellow, as Verlie is). His eyes are big and brown, but dragged downward with his inside sickness. And his sadness: he is a lonesome man, almost out of luck.

❧❦❧

"Whatever do you suppose they talk about?" Tom

15

Todd says to Jessica, who has come into his study to help him with the index of his book, an hour or so after breakfast. They can hear the slow, quiet sounds of Verlie's voice, with Clifton's, from the kitchen.

"Us, maybe?" Jessica makes this light, attempting a joke, but she really wonders if in fact she and Tom are their subject. Her own communication with Verlie is so mystifyingly nonverbal that she sometimes suspects Verlie of secret (and accurate) appraisals, as though Verlie knows her in ways that no one else does, herself included. At other times she thinks that Verlie is just plain stubborn.

From the window come spring breaths of blossom and grasses and leaves. Of spring earth. Aging plump Jessica deeply sighs.

Tom says, "I very much doubt that, my dear. Incredibly fascinating though we be."

In near total despair Jessica says, "Sometimes I think I just don't have the feeling for an index."

The telephone rings. Tom and Jessica look at each other, and then Verlie's face comes to the study door. "It's for you, Mr. Todd. A long distance."

❧

Clifton has had a bad life; it almost seems cursed. The same sickness one spring down in Mississippi carried off his wife and three poor little children, and after that everything got even worse: every job that he got came apart like a bunch of sticks in his hands. Folks all said that they had no money to pay. He even made deliveries for a bootlegger, knocking on back doors at night, but the man got arrested and sent to jail before Clifton got any money.

He likes working for the Todds, and at the few other jobs around town that Mrs. Todd finds for him. But he doesn't feel good. Sometimes he thinks he has some kind of sickness.

He looks anxiously at Verlie as he says this last, as though he, like Jessica, believes that she can see inside him.

"You nervous," Verlie says. "You be all right, come summertime." But she can't look at him as she says this.

They are standing in the small apple orchard where Verlie's clotheslines are. She has been hanging out the sheets. They billow, shuddering in the lively restive air of early spring.

Clifton suddenly takes hold of her face, and turns it around to his. He presses his mouth and his body to hers, standing there. Something deep inside Verlie heats up and makes her almost melt.

"Verlie!"

It is Avery, suddenly coming up on them, so that they cumbersomely step apart.

"Verlie, my father wants you." Avery runs away almost before she has stopped speaking.

Clifton asks, "You reckon we ought to tell her not to tell?"

"No, she's not going to tell."

Verlie is right, but it is a scene that Avery thinks about. Of course, she has seen other grown-ups kissing: her father and Irene McGinnis or someone after a party. But Verlie and Clifton looked different; for one thing they were more absorbed. It took them a long time to hear her voice.

❧

Tom is desperately questioning Jessica. "How in God's name will I tell her?" he asks.

Verlie's husband, Horace, is dead. He died in a

17

Memphis hospital, after a knife fight, having first told a doctor the name of the people and the town where his wife worked.

"I could tell her," Jessica forces herself to say, and for a few minutes they look at each other, with this suggestion lying between them. But they both know, with some dark and intimate Southern knowledge, that Tom will have to be the one to tell her. And alone: it would not even "do" for Jessica to stay on in the room, although neither of them could have explained these certainties.

❦

Having been clearly (and kindly) told by Tom what has happened in Memphis, Verlie then asks, "You sure? You sure it's Horace, not any other man?"

Why couldn't he have let Jessica tell her, or at least have let her stay in the room? Tom in uncomfortable; it wildly occurs to him to offer Verlie a drink (to offer Verlie a drink?). He mumbles, "Yes, I'm afraid there's no doubt at all." He adds, in his more reasonable, professorial voice, "You see, another man wouldn't have said Verlie Jones, who works for the Todd family, in Hilton."

Incredibly, a smile breaks out on Verlie's face. ("For a minute I actually thought she was going to *laugh*," Tom later says to Jessica.)

Verlie says, "I reckon that's right. Couldn't be no other man." And then she says, "Lunch about ready now," and she goes back into the kitchen.

Jessica has been hovering in the dining room, pushing at the arrangement of violets and cowslips in a silver bowl. She follows Verlie into the kitchen; she says, "Verlie, I'm terribly sorry. Verlie, wouldn't you like to go on home? Take the afternoon off. I could drive you . . ."

"No'm. No, thank you. I'd liefer get on with the ironing."

And so, with a stiff and unreadable face, opaque dark-brown eyes, Verlie serves their lunch.

❧

What could they know, what could any of them know about a man like Horace? Had any of them seen her scars? Knife scars and beating scars, and worse things he had done without leaving any scars. All the time he forced her, when he was so hurting and quick, and she was sick or just plain exhausted. The girls she always knew he had. The mean tricks he played on little kids, his kids. The dollars of hers that he stole to get drunk on.

She had always thought Horace was too mean to die, and as she cleans up the lunch dishes and starts to sprinkle the dry sheets for ironing, she still wonders: *Is Horace dead?*

She tries to imagine an open casket, full of Horace, dead. His finicky little moustache and his long, strong fingers folded together on his chest. But the casket floats off into the recesses of her mind and what she sees is Horace, alive and terrifying.

A familiar dry smell tells her that she has scorched a sheet, and tears begin to roll slowly down her face.

❧

"When I went into the kitchen to see how she was, she was standing there with tears rolling down her face," Jessica reports to Tom—and then is appalled at what she hears as satisfaction in her own voice.

"I find that hardly surprising," Tom says, with a questioning raise of his eyebrows.

Aware that she has lost his attention, Jessica goes on.

(Where *is* he—with whom?) "I just meant, it seems awful to feel a sort of relief when she cries. As though I thought that's what she ought to do. Maybe she didn't really care for Horace. He hasn't been around for years, after all." (As usual she is making things worse: it is apparent that Tom can barely listen.)

She says, "I think I'll take the index cards back to my desk," and she manages not to cry.

❦

Picking up the sheets to take upstairs to the linen closet, Verlie decides that she won't tell Clifton about Horace; dimly she thinks that if she tells anyone, especially Clifton, it won't be true: Horace, alive, will be waiting for her at her house, as almost every night she is afraid that he will be.

❦

Sitting at her desk, unseeingly Jessica looks out across the deep valley, where the creek winds down toward the sea, to the further hills that are bright green with spring. Despair slowly fills her blood so that it seems heavy in her veins, and thick, and there is a heavy pressure in her head.

And she dreams for a moment, as she has sometimes before, of a friend to whom she could say, "I can't stand anything about my life. My husband either is untrue to me or would like to be—constantly. It comes to the same thing, didn't St. Paul say that? My daughter's eyes are beginning to go cold against me, and my son is terrified of everyone. Of me." But there is no one to whom she could say a word of this; she is known among her friends for dignity and restraint. (Only sometimes her mind explodes, and she breaks out screaming—at Tom, at one of her children, once at

Verlie—leaving them all sick and shocked, especially herself sick and shocked, and further apart than ever.)

Now Verlie comes through the room with an armful of fresh, folded sheets, and for an instant, looking at her, Jessica has the thought that Verlie could be that friend, that listener. That Verlie could understand.

She dismisses the impulse almost as quickly as it came.

Lately she has spent a lot of time remembering college, those distant happy years, among friends. Her successes of that time. The two years when she directed the Greek play, on May Day weekend (really better than being in the May Court). Her senior year, elected president of the secret honor society. (And the springs of wisteria, heavily flowering, scented, lavender and white, the heavy vines everywhere.)

From those college days she still has two friends, to whom she writes, and visits at rarer intervals. Elizabeth, who is visibly happily married to handsome and successful Jackson Stuart (although he is, to Jessica, a shocking racial bigot). And Mary John James, who teaches Latin in a girls' school, in Richmond—who has never married. Neither of them could be her imagined friend (any more than Verlie could).

❧

Not wanting to see Jessica's sad eyes again (the sorrow in that woman's face, the mourning!), Verlie puts the sheets in the linen closet and goes down the back stairs. She is halfway down, walking slow, when she feels a sudden coolness in her blood, as though from a breeze. She stops, she listens to nothing and then she is flooded with the certain knowledge that Horace is dead, is at that very moment laid away in Memphis (wherever Memphis is). Standing there alone, by the halfway window that looks out to the giant rhododendron, she begins to smile, peacefully and slowly—an interior, pervasive smile.

Then she goes on down the stairs, through the dining room and into the kitchen.

Clifton is there.

Her smile changes; her face becomes brighter and more animated, although she doesn't say anything—not quite trusting herself not to say everything, as she has promised herself.

"You looking perky," Clifton says, by way of a question. He is standing at the sink with a drink of water.

Her smile broadens, and she lies. "Thinking about the social at the church. Just studying if or not I ought to go."

"You do right to go," he says. And then, "You be surprise, you find me there?"

(They have never arranged any meeting before, much less in another place, at night; they have always pretended that they were in the same place in the yard or orchard by accident.)

She laughs. "You never find the way."

He grins at her, his face brighter than any face that she has ever seen. "I be there," he says to her.

❦

A long, hot summer, extending into fall. A hot October, and then there is sudden cold. Splinters of frost on the red clay erosions in the fields. Ice in the shallow edges of the creek.

For Verlie it has been the happiest summer of her life, but no one of the Todds has remarked on this, nor been consciously aware of unusual feelings, near at hand. They all have preoccupations of their own.

Clifton has been working for the Macombers, friends and neighbors of the Todds, and it is Irene Macomber who telephones to tell Jessica the sad news that he had a kind of seizure (a hemorrhage) and that when they finally got him to the Negro hospital (twelve miles away) it was too late, and he died.

Depressing news, on that dark November day. Jessica supposes that the first thing is to tell Verlie. (After all, she and Clifton were friends, and Verlie might know of relatives.)

She is not prepared for Verlie's reaction.

A wail—"Aieeeee"—that goes on and on, from Verlie's wide mouth, and her wide, wild eyes. "Aieee—"

Then it stops abruptly, as Verlie claps her hands over her mouth, and bends over and blindly reaches for a chair, her rocker. She pulls herself toward the chair, she falls into it, she bends over double and begins to cough, deep and wrackingly.

Poor shocked Jessica has no notion what to do. To go over to Verlie and embrace her, to press her own sorrowing face to Verlie's face? To creep shyly and sadly from the room?

This last is what she does—is all, perhaps, that she is able to do.

❧

"You know," says Tom Todd (seriously) to Irene McGinnis, in one of their rare lapses from the steady demands of unconsummated love, "I believe those two people had a real affection for each other."

❧

Verlie is sick for a week and more after that, with what is called "misery in the chest." (No one mentions her heart.)

Thinking to amuse her children (she is clearly at a

23

loss without Verlie, and she knows this), Jessica takes them for a long walk, on the hard, narrow, white roads that lead up into the hills, the heavy, thick, dark woods of fall, smelling of leaves and earth and woodsmoke. But a melancholy mood settles over them all; it is cold and the children are tired, and Jessica finds that she is thinking of Verlie and Clifton. (Is it possible that they were lovers? She uncomfortably shrugs off this possibility.)

Dark comes early, and there is a raw, red sunset at the black edge of the horizon, as finally they reach home.

Verlie comes back the next day, to everyone's relief. But there is a grayish tinge to the color of her skin that does not go away.

❦

But on that rare spring day months earlier (the day Horace is dead and laid away in Memphis) Verlie walks the miles home with an exceptional lightness of heart, smiling to herself at all the colors of the bright new flowers, and at the smells of spring, the promises.

THE TODDS

Are You in Love?

"But I absolutely can't understand Mr. Auden," says Jessica Todd, curiously flirtatious. She is speaking to Linton Wheeler, a much younger man, a student and himself a poet. They are in Jessica's bookstore, in a small university town: Hilton, in the middle South. She is seated behind her desk. Small and plump, with little shape, sad, not aging well, Jessica usually thinks of herself (she *feels* herself) in terms of defects (pores and sags), but today she is aware only of her eyes, which are large and dark brown. Even Tom, her husband, has said that they are beautiful. She and Linton are communicating through their eyes, hers to his wide-spaced hazel. Eyes and somewhat similar voices—both are from Virginia.

"Or Delmore Schwartz or T. S. Eliot either," says Jessica, with an exaggerated sigh.

Serious Linton begins to explain. William Empson, Brooks and Warren. He mentions Donne and the Metaphysicals. Jacobean drama. Pound?

"You *know* I can't read Ezra Pound."

Linton's skin is very fair, even now, in midsummer; he dislikes the sun, stays indoors. His hair is a light sandy brown, worn longer than the fashion of that time (middle Thirties). There are Bacchus curls around his face. A wide mouth, with curiously flat lips. Jessica has sometimes imagined that the young Shelley looked like that. She spent her girlhood reading Shelley, and Byron and Keats and Wordsworth, but especially Shelley, and she has wondered if she married Tom Todd because he was—still is, in fact—writing a book on Shelley. (Not true: she married him because of passionate kisses— then.)

"You really should try to read Brooks and Warren," says gentle Linton, now.

"Oh, Linton, I will, I really will." And for no reason, but happily, she laughs.

Earlier they have both been laughing at other customers who have been in and out, habitués of Jessica's: Clarissa Noble, who can't remember which mystery stories she's already read; old Mrs. Vain, who only reads books on genealogy or gardening; Dr. Willingham, the filthy-minded botanist; Miss Phipps, a blond beautician, who likes love stories with nice endings.

Good friends, Jessica and Linton, despite a gap in age, laughing together in the middle of a summer afternoon.

The store is a narrow, very high-ceilinged building, with windows up near the roof, through which now slanting downward come bright bars of light, moted with dust, in the otherwise dim and book-crowded room. Next door is the Presbyterian church, red brick, with a formal hedged green yard. Tom is, or was, a Presbyterian, but Jessica is an almost lapsed Episcopalian. (Not quite: those prayers and especially the General Confession linger in her mind and at odd times they surface.) She and Tom have never gone to church, to either church, and it seems an irony to Jessica that his church (of which she faintly disapproves: that dismal catechism) should be next door to her store.

Linton smokes too much. He always smells of cigarettes; he leaves in his wake a drift of stale smoke. He blows smoke out, then leans back and inhales it, in a way that Jessica has never seen anyone inhale. A shy boy, from a very small town—a country crossroads—this way of smoking is perhaps his boldest gesture.

He likes Jessica, or, rather, he does not *not* like her, as he does most older women. Of young ones, the coeds, he is simply and absolutely terrified.

"I've always loved poetry," says Jessica. "But these new things—it isn't fair." She feels curiously giddy.

One of the things that Linton likes about Jessica is that she doesn't dye her hair, as his mother does. At that moment he can hardly see her face, in that dim light, but a bar of sunlight has reached her head, turning white to gold. "Ma'am, you do have the prettiest hair," says Linton shyly.

"Why, Linton—" Tears rush toward her eyes—her heart might break. "Why, Linton, what a very sweet thing to say," she barely gets out.

Should he not have said that? Sensing strong emotion, which he imagines to be distress, Linton retreats to poetry. "And *Seven Types of Ambiguity*, that's really something, ma'am," he says, blushing. "I know you'd enjoy that one."

"I'll try it." Jessica speaks faintly, wishing he would go: she would like to be alone, to savor and to think.

"My goodness, it's almost five," says Linton. "I've got to get to work." He is a part-time waiter at the college cafeteria, Swain Hall, which is inevitably called Swine Hall. Linton is what is called a self-help student.

He half smiles, and hurries out, banging the old door and letting in a wave of exhausted late-afternoon summer air. Leaving his stale Camel smell.

Motionless, Jessica sits there smiling. She is almost dazzled by her sudden sharp (if narrow) glimpse of possibilities, a bright glimpse like a slit in the darkness of her usual melancholy. She is a woman not yet forty with beautiful eyes. And beautiful hair. Linton is not a possibility. (Is he?) But older women, especially literary women, sometimes have young men, Young Lovers. A woman desired is a woman not seen as herself, is a woman re-created—she is remembering Tom's brief blind passion for her.

To be loved by a much younger person is to be forgiven, forgiven for age. Did she read that somewhere? Did she make it up?

Still smiling, she shakes her head, to shake off all of this. But she is aware of a rare mood of indulgence toward herself. She knows that it is silly, this imagining of young lovers, at her age. But on the other hand— why not? Is love restricted to people of a definite age, and a certain degree of beauty?

(Yes, indeed it is, she is later to decide, and she is to feel, as she has felt before, that her own needs, insofar as they are sexual, are obscene. *But Thou, O Lord, have mercy upon us miserable offenders.*)

She puts the money from the cashbox into her purse, $5.73; she stands up and looks around. She walks determinedly toward the door, which she opens and closes and locks behind her.

Her car, the old Chevy, is parked at the curb. For a wonder, it starts up easily. She drives down Main Street, turns left at the light and heads out of town, toward her own house.

It is a lovely afternoon, and the town just now is at its greenest and loveliest. The lawns, the profuse shrubbery, the heavy green pine boughs against a barely fading pale-blue sky—all beautiful. Jessica drives down the long white concrete highway, the last hill leading home, with an obscure anticipation.

Her own driveway leads to the back of the house, past the old terraced garden, the abandoned tennis court. Roses, just past their prime, climb the fence at the far edge of the garden, and the grape arbor is flowing with green vines. At the moment Jessica is in love with her house, the land, their garden.

◈

Beyond the side yard some woods begin, pines and maples, cedars, elms; through these trees is the path leading down to the swimming pool (Tom's pride, built with his World War I bonus, and partly with his own hands). That is where Tom and the children will be. Probably with some company.

Jessica goes inside the house, and upstairs to her room to change into her bathing suit. Undressing, she does not regard her body in the long mirror or think about it, as she sometimes does (unhappily). Humming something to herself, she puts on her dark wool suit, her flowered beige kimona, slippers, and she picks up her white rubber cap from the top of her chest of drawers, the mahogany chest that matches the broad double bed, which her parents slept in, in Virginia. Tom has moved into what was meant to be the guest room.

She goes downstairs, still humming, through the living room and out the side door, down to the lawn. She smiles as she recognizes that the tune is an Easter hymn—"There Is a Green Hill Far Away"—Easter songs, in August? But something in the air that day has more of spring than summer in it, some fragrance, some suggestion.

Should she invite Linton to come over for a swim sometime? Well, why not?

At the edge of the woods, the top of the embedded slate steps that lead down to the pool, she pauses and listens, separating out voices. Tom's—his laugh. The somewhat higher responding laugh of Harry McGinnis, there with his wife, Irene. And at the prospect of Irene, of watching Irene with Tom, Jessica's breath tightens in a way that is drearily familiar to her, but then she thinks a new thought: she thinks, So what?—for her an unfamiliar phrase. So what? Tom has a crush on Irene, and she on him. So what? Today, at this moment, her own heart is light and high. Is indestructible?

She starts down the path, and halfway down, just past the giant maple in which her children have built a tree-house, she calls out, "Here I am! Hello?" She is unaware of sounding not quite like herself. As though she were a guest?

She is answered by silence, a break in whatever they were laughing about, and then Tom's voice: "Well, old dear, so at long last you're home?"

They are all there, as she descends to the clearing: Tom (her Tom), tall and slender, blue-eyed, censorious; Harry, dark and slight, neatly made; and pretty blond Irene, in a ruffled pink bathing suit. And children: her own thin two, dark Avery, and fairer Devlin, on a steamer rug, on the grass; and young Harry McGinnis, who lies tensely on the edge of the pool, in a space of sun. Harry is a golden boy, extremely handsome—almost beautiful, looking like neither Irene nor his father.

For something to say, Jessica calls out, "Children, you look cold, you wrap up in your towels. Avery, Devlin." They look at her with blank and patient faces, and then Avery turns toward young Harry, who has begun to do pushups, there beside the pool.

Jessica says, "Why, Irene, what a pretty bathing suit. Can you really wear it into the water?"

Before Irene can answer Tom breaks in, "That's what she alleges, but we have yet to see a test of her claim, any proof of her alleged bathing suit." He makes a gesture as though to throw her into the pool.

And Irene turns from Jessica to Tom. "You wouldn't!" she cries out. "You're just a mean old tease, Tom Todd. Of course I can swim in this suit, it's just that I'm feeling so warm, and so lazy."

"Tom, darling, I'm dying for a drink," says Jessica. "What a perfect day for gin." (Again she sounds like someone else, but who? Someone in a book?) "But first I'll go in for a little dip," she says. This is herself; it is what she always says, and does.

Dropping her robe, as no one watches, she steps into the shallow end of the rough concrete oval; as the cool sliding water reaches her waist she begins to swim a gentle breaststroke, her legs in a practiced frog kick, to the end of the pool. There she reaches for the edge, and, holding on, she looks back at the group in the clearing, in the sun, who are not watching her. Harry (big Harry: this distinction is to become ironic in a few years, when his son grows so much larger than he), big Harry is telling a story; Jessica can catch echoes of his precise and somewhat finicky voice, not quite hearing what he says.

Tom is looking at Irene, so small and blond, preening herself in the sun, in Tom's gaze. And Jessica wonders how that would be, to be a woman looked at by men, aware of the power of one's face, one's small and desirable body. She can't imagine it, and she lets go of the end of the pool, to swim back slowly, in the cool and concealing water.

She gets out quickly, and in a single gesture she picks up and puts on her robe. Elaborately Tom hands her the drink that he has made for her. His gestures always seem to mock themselves. (Is Jessica for the first time observing this? She has a sense of heightened powers, of newly and acutely sensing what is around her.)

Harry McGinnis is a Classics professor, which was Jessica's field of concentration at Randolph-Macon, and he sometimes teases her about what he terms her desertion, her flight to modernity. He also teases her about what he calls her radical ideas; he says that

Negroes have smaller brains than white people, making Jessica furious—but does he mean it? No one knows, least of all Jessica.

Today, which is all around an odd day, she decides to tease Harry. Well, why not? (So what?) "Well, Harry," she begins, "I've just spent the most wonderful morning reading Mrs. Virginia Woolf. Of course you couldn't be persuaded to read any lady after Sappho?"

Pleased—he enjoys a little argument, although he has the Southern male's generations-deep distrust of intelligence in women—Harry responds with more than usual gallantry: "Well, if anyone could persuade me, it would be you, Miss Jessica."

Staring at the neat brown patch of hair on his chest, Jessica is wondering where to go from there when Tom breaks in: "Speaking of modernity," he somewhat loudly says (is that what they were talking about?), "have you good people heard the news that Benny Goodman is going to play in Carnegie Hall? Ben-ny Good-man." His isolation of each syllable is replete with contempt.

Anti-Semitic. This horrifying word, or perception (which is not entirely new: from time to time he has said certain not nice things about his Jewish students), enters Jessica's mind, and it is in fact so horrifying that she must force it out (Hitler, Jews in Germany—of course Tom is not like that). Defensively she says, "I really can't see what's so terrible about that."

Lifting his head, for one instant Tom glares as though Jessica were a student (a Jewish student?) and then he turns to Harry and he says, "Jessica really only likes hymns. Episcopal hymns, of course. She's always humming them, although a little off-key." And he laughs, as though he had spoken kindly, or even amusingly.

Turning from him (something unbearable has risen in her chest), Jessica looks over toward her children.

Devlin is still there on the steamer rug, a towel obediently draped around his shoulders, but Avery has got up and walked around to the side of the pool, where young Harry is lying in the sun. She squats there beside him, much less beautiful than he; she seems to be saying something, but whatever it is Harry does not answer, nor even turn toward her. *Avery is in love with Harry*. Blindingly, Jessica sees and feels this, as at the same time she tells herself that it is absolutely impossible: Avery is only nine, many years too young for a feeling of that sort. Impossible.

"Ben-ny Good-man," Tom says again. "What do you imagine he'll play—'The Flight of the Bumblebee'?"

"Silly, you're thinking of Jack Benny." Irene laughs, tinklingly.

"Well, I suppose I should concede that there is some difference between them." Tom draws in his chin, raising his head in a characteristic gesture of defiance. But then, since it was Irene who spoke, he turns aside and allows his stern expression to dissolve into a laugh.

But suddenly, then, there is a tremendous sound, an explosion of water. All the grown-ups turn to see young Harry floundering in the pool—to see Avery, who has evidently just pushed him in, whose face is terrified, appalled.

Everyone screams at once—everyone but Jessica and Avery, who are staring at each other, frozen, across the pool.

Young Harry, from the pool to Avery: "You little bitch—"

Tom: "Avery, how dare you, *damn* you—"

Irene: "Harry, honey, your stomach's all scraped—"

Big Harry to his son: "Don't you ever let me hear you use language like that, and to a girl—"

At the sound of that spash something within Jessica has itself exploded, the day has exploded, and for a moment she is immobilized (as Avery is). Jessica hears

33

all those shouts as though they were distant voices. But then in a rush she gets up and hurries around to where Avery is, Avery still standing beside the pool, beside the place where Harry was lying. Jessica grasps her daughter's arm. She pulls her around to the other side of the pool and then up the twig- and pebble-strewn slate steps, almost dragging her along, toward the side yard and the house.

Where the lawn begins Jessica stops; she turns to face Avery and to grasp her shoulders. And she begins to shake her daughter, saying loudly, terribly, "What's the matter with you, are you in love with Harry McGinnis? *Are you in love?*"

Shaking her until they are both weeping.

THE TODDS

Alternatives

It is the summer of 1935, and there are two people sitting at the end of a porch. The house is in Maine, at the edge of a high bluff that overlooks a large and for the moment peaceful lake. Tom Todd and Barbara Rutherford. They have recently met. (She and her husband are houseguests of the Todds.) They laugh a lot, they are terribly excited about each other and they have no idea what to do with what they feel. She is a very blond, bright-eyed girl in her twenties, wearing very short white shorts, swinging long thin legs below the high hammock on which she is perched, looking down at Tom. He is a fair, slender man with sad lines beside his mouth, but not now! Now he is laughing with Babs. Some ten years older than she, he is a professor, writing a book on Shelley (O wild West Wind), but the Depression has had unhappy effects on his university (Hilton, in the middle South): 10 percent salary cuts, cancellation of sabbaticals. He is unable to finish his book (no promotion); they rely more and more on his wife's small income from her bookstore. And he himself has been depressed—but not now. What a girl, this Babs!

The house itself is old, with weathered shingles that once were green, and its shape is peculiar; it used to be the central lodge for a camp for underprivileged girls that Jessica Todd owned and ran before her marriage to Tom. The large, high living room is still full of souvenirs from that era: group pictures of girls in bloomers and middies, who danced or, rather, posed in discreet Greek tunics, and wore headbands; and over the fireplace, just below a moldering deer's head, there is a mouse-nibbled triangular felt banner, once dark green, that announced the name of the camp: Wabuwana. Why does Jessica keep all those things around, as though those were her happiest days? No one ever asked. Since there were no bedrooms, Tom and Jessica slept in a curtained-off alcove, with not much privacy; two very small rooms that once were storage closets are bedrooms for their children, Avery and Devlin. Babs and her husband, Wilfred Rutherford, have been put in a tent down the path, on one of a row of gray plank tent floors where all the camper girls used to sleep. Babs said, "How absolutely divine—I've never slept in a tent." "You haven't?" Jessica asked. "I think I sleep best in tents."

A narrow screened-in porch runs the length of the house, and there is a long table out there—too long for just the four Todds, better (less lonely) with even two guests. The porch widens at its end, making a sort of round room, where Tom and Babs now are, not looking at the view.

Around the house there are clumps of hemlocks, tall Norway pines, white pines, and birches that bend out from the high bank. Across the smooth bright lake are the White Mountains, the Presidential Range—sharp blue Mount Adams and farther back, in the exceptionally clear days of early fall, such as this day is, you can see Mount Washington silhouetted. Lesser, gentler slopes take up the foreground: Mount Pleasant, Douglas Hill.

Beside Babs in the hammock lies a ukulele—hers, which Tom wants her to play.

"Oh, but I'm no good at *all*," she protests. "Wilfred can't stand it when I play!"

"I'll be able to stand it, I can promise you that, my dear."

Her accent is very Bostonian, his Southern; both tendencies seem to intensify as they talk together.

She picks up the instrument, plucks the four strings as she sings, "My dog has fleas."

"So does Louise," he sings mockingly, an echo. Tom is fond of simple ridiculous jokes but he feels it necessary always to deliver them as though someone else were talking. In fact, he says almost everything indirectly.

They both laugh, looking at each other.

They are still laughing when Jessica comes out from the living room where she has been reading (every summer she rereads Jane Austen) and walks down the length of the porch to where they are, and says, "Oh, a ukulele, how nice, Barbara. Some of our girls used to play."

Chivalrous Tom gets up to offer his chair—"Here you are, old dear." She did not want to sit so close to the hammock but does anyway, a small shapeless woman on the edge of her chair.

Jessica is only a few years older than Tom but she looks considerably more so, with graying hair and sad brown eyes, a tightly compressed mouth. She has strong and definite Anglo-Saxon notions about good behavior. (They all do, this helpless group of American Protestants, Tom and Jessica, Barbara and Wilfred, which they try and almost succeed in passing on to their children.) Jessica wears no makeup and is dressed in what she calls "camp clothes," meaning things that are old and shabby (what she thinks she deserves). "Won't you play something for us?" she asks Babs.

"Perhaps you will succeed in persuasion where I have failed," says Tom. As he sees it, his chief duty toward his wife is to be unfailingly polite, and he always is, although sometimes it comes across a little heavily.

Of course Jessica feels the currents between Babs and Tom but she accepts what she senses with melancholy resignation. There is a woman at home whom Tom likes too, small, blond Irene McGinnis, and Irene is crazy about Tom—that's clear—but nothing happens. Sometimes they kiss; Jessica has noticed that Verlie always hides Tom's handkerchiefs. Verlie also likes Tom. Nothing more will happen with Babs. It is only mildly depressing for Jessica, a further reminder that she is an aging, not physically attractive woman, and that her excellent mind is not compelling to Tom. But she is used to all that. She sighs, and says, "I think there's going to be a very beautiful sunset," and she looks across the lake to the mountains. "There's Mount Washington," she says.

Then the porch door bangs open and Wilfred walks toward them, a heavy, dark young man with sleeves rolled up over big hairy arms; he has been washing and polishing his new Ford. He is a distant cousin of Jessica's. "Bab's, you're not going to play that thing, are you?"

"No, darling, I absolutely promise."

"Well," Tom says, "surely it's time for a drink?"

"It surely is," says Babs, giggling, mocking him.

He gestures as though to slap at the calf of her long leg, but of course he does not; his hand stops some inches away.

Down a wide pine-needled path, some distance from the lodge, there is a decaying birchbark canoe, inside which white Indian pipes grow. They were planted years back by the camper girls. Around the canoe stands a grove of pines with knotted roots, risen up from the ground, in which chipmunks live. Feeding the chipmunks is what Jessica and Tom's children do when they aren't swimming or playing on the beach. Avery and Devlin in their skimpy shorts sit crosslegged on the pine needles, making clucking noises to bring out the chipmunks.

A small chipmunk comes out, bright-eyed, switching his tail back and forth, looking at the children, but then he scurries off.

Devlin asks, "Do you like Babs?" He underlines the name, meaning that he thinks it's silly.

"She's O.K." Avery's voice is tight; she is confused by Babs. She doesn't know whether to think, as her mother probably does, that Babs's white shorts are too short, that she is too dressed up in her pink silk shirt for camp, or to be pleased at the novel sort of attention she gets from Babs, who said last night at dinner, "You know, Avery, when you're a little older you should have an evening dress this color," and pointed to the flame-gold gladioli on the table, in a gray stone crock.

"Her shorts are too short," says Devlin.

"What do you know about clothes? They're supposed to be short—*shorts*." Saying this, for a moment Avery feels that she *is* Babs, who wears lipstick and anything she wants to, whom everyone looks at.

"Mother doesn't wear shorts, ever."

"So what? You think she's well dressed?"

Devlin is appalled; he has no idea what to make of what she has said. "I'll tell!" He is desperate. "I'll tell her what you said."

"Just try, you silly little sissy. Come on, I'll race you to the lodge."

Both children scramble up, Avery first, of course, and run across the slippery pines, their skinny brown legs flashing between the trees, and arrive at the house together and slam open the screen door and tear down the length of the porch to the cluster of grown-ups.

"Mother, do you know what Avery said?"

"No, darling, but please don't tell me unless it was something very amusing." This is out of character for Jessica, and Devlin stares at his mother, who strokes his light hair, and says, "Now, let's all be quiet. Barbara is going to play a song."

Babs picks up her ukulele and looks down at it as she begins her song, which turns out to be a long ballad about a lonely cowboy and a pretty city girl. She has an attractive, controlled alto voice. She becomes more and more sure of herself as she goes along, and sometimes looks up and smiles around at the group—at Tom—as she sings.

Tom has an exceptional ear, as well as a memory for words; somewhere, sometime, he has heard that ballad before, so that by the time she reaches the end he is singing with her, and they reach the last line together, looking into each other's eyes with a great stagy show of exaggeration; they sing together, "And they loved forevermore."

But they are not, that night, lying hotly together on the cold beach, furiously kissing, wildly touching everywhere. That happens only in Tom's mind as he lies next to Jessica and hears her soft sad snores. In her cot, in the tent, Babs sleeps very soundly, as she always does, and she dreams of the first boy she ever kissed, whose name was not Tom.

☙⟊❧

Some years later, almost the same group gathers for dinner around a large white restaurant table, the Buon Gusto, in San Francisco. There are Tom and Jessica, and Babs, but she is without Wilfred, whom she has just divorced in Reno. Devlin is there. Devlin grown plump and sleek, smug with his new job of supervising window display at the City of Paris. Avery is there, with her second husband, Stanley.

Tom and Barbara have spent the afternoon in bed together, in her hotel room—that old love finally consummated. They are both violently aware of the afternoon behind them; they are partly still there, together in the tangled sea-smelling sheets. Barbara presses her legs close. Tom wonders if there is any smell of her on him that anyone could notice.

No one notices anything; they all have problems of their own.

In the more than ten years since they were all in Maine, Jessica has sunk further into her own painful and very private despair. She is not fatter, but her body has lost all definition, and her clothes are deliberately middle-aged, as though she were eager to be done with being a sexual woman. Her melancholy eyes are large, terribly dark; below them her cheeks sag, and the corners of her mouth have a small sad downward turn. Tom is always carrying on—the phrase she uses to herself—with someone or other; she has little energy left with which to care. But sometimes, still, a lively rebellious voice within her cries out that it is all cruelly unfair; she has done everything that she was taught a wife is expected to do; she has kept house and cared for children and listened to Tom, laughed at his jokes and never said no when he felt like making love—done all those things, been a faithful and quiet wife when often she didn't want to at all, and there he is, unable to keep his eyes off Babs, laughing at all *her* jokes.

Tom has promised Barbara that he will leave Jessica; this winter they will get a divorce, and he will apply for a teaching job at Stanford or U.C., and he and Babs will live in San Francisco; they are both in love with the city.

Avery has recently begun psychoanalysis with a very

orthodox Freudian; he says nothing, and she becomes more and more hysterical—she is lost! And now this untimely visit from her parents; agonized, she questions them about events of her early childhood, as though to get her bearings. "Was I nine or ten when I had whooping cough?"

"What?" says Jessica, who had daringly been embarked on an alternate version of her own life in which she did not marry Tom but instead went on to graduate school herself, and took a doctorate in Classics. (But who would have hired a woman professor in the Twenties?) "Tom, I'd love another drink," she says. "Barbara? You too?" Late in her life Jessica has discovered the numbing effects of drink—you can sleep!

"Oh, yes, divine."

Sipping what was still his first vermouth, Devlin repeats to himself that most women are disgusting. He excepts his mother. He is sitting next to Babs, and he cannot stand her perfume, which is Joy.

Looking at Jessica, whom, curiously, she has always liked, Barbara feels a chill in her heart. Are they doing the right thing, she and Tom? He says they are; he says Jessica has her bookstore and her student poet friends ("Fairies, most of them, from the look of them," Tom says), and that living with him does not make her happy at all; he has never made her happy. Is he only talking to himself, rationalizing? Barbara doesn't know.

All these people, so many of them Southern, make Avery's husband, Stanley, feel quite lost; in fact, he finds it hard to understand anything they say. Tom is especially opaque: the heavy Southern accent and heavier irony combine to creat confusion, which is perhaps what Tom intends. Stanley thinks Tom is a little crazy, and feels great sympathy for Jessica, whom he admires. And he thinks, Poor Avery, growing up in all that—no wonder Devlin's queer and Avery has to go to a shrink. Stanley feels an awful guilt toward Avery, for not supplying all that Tom and Jessica failed to give her, and for his persistent "premature ejaculations"—and putting the phrase in quotes is not much help.

"I remember your whooping cough very well indeed," says Tom, pulling in his chin so that the back of his head jerks up; it is a characteristic gesture, an odd combination of self-mockery and self-congratulation. "It was the same summer you pushed Harry McGinnis into the swimming pool." He turns to Stanley, who is as incomprehensible to him as he is to Stanley, but he tries. "Odd gesture, that. Her mother and I thought she had a sort of 'crush' on young Harry, and then she went and pushed him into the pool." He chuckles. "Don't try to tell me that ladies aren't creatures of whim, even twelve-year-old girls."

"I was nine," says Avery, and does not add, You had a crush on Harry's mother, you were crazy about Irene that summer.

Jessica thinks the same thing, and she and Avery are both looking at Tom, so that he feels the thought.

"I remember teasing Irene about the bathing suit she wore that day," he says recklessly, staring about with his clear blue eyes at the unfamiliar room.

"What was it like?" asks Barbara, very interested.

"Oh, some sort of ruffled thing. You know how those Southern gals are," he says, clearly not meaning either his wife or his daughter.

"I must have thought the whooping cough was a sort of punishment," Avery says. "For having a crush on Harry, as you put it."

"Yes, probably," Jessica agrees, being herself familiar with many varieties of guilt. "You were awful sick—it was terrible. There was nothing we could do."

"When was the first summer you came to Maine?" Devlin asks Babs, coldly curious, nearly rude. It is plain that he wishes she never had.

"Nineteen thirty-five. In September. In fact September 9th," she says, and then blushes for the accuracy of her recall, and looks at Tom.

"Verlie took care of me," says Avery, still involved with her whooping cough.

Jessica sighs deeply. "Yes, I suppose she did."

❦

Almost ten years later, in the middle Fifties, Tom and Barbara are married. In the chapel of the little church, the Swedenborgian, in San Francisco, both their faces stream with tears as the minister says those words.

In her forties, Barbara is a striking woman still, with her small disdainful nose, her sleekly knotted pale hair, and her beautiful way of walking, holding herself forward like a present. She has aged softly, as very fine-skinned, very blond women sometimes do. And Tom is handsome still; they make a handsome couple (they always have).

Avery is there; she reflects that she is now older than Barbara was in 1935, that summer in Maine. She is almost thirty, divorced from Stanley, and disturbingly in love with two men at once. Has Barbara never loved anyone but Tom? (Has she?) Avery sees their tears as highly romantic.

She herself is a nervy, attractive girl with emphatic dark eyebrows, large dark eyes and a friendly soft mouth, heavy breasts on an otherwise slender body. She wishes she had not worn her black silk suit, despite its chic; two friends have assured her that no one thought about wearing black to weddings anymore, but now it seems a thing not to have done. "I wore black to my father's wedding"—thank God she is not still seeing Dr. Gunderscheim, and will use that sentence only as a joke. Mainly, Avery is wondering which of the two men

44

to marry, Charles or Christopher. (The slight similarity of the names seems ominous—what does it mean?) This wondering is a heavy obsessive worry to her; it drags at her mind, pulling it down. Now for the first time, in the small dim chapel, candelit, it wildly occurs to her that perhaps she should marry neither of them, perhaps she should not marry at all, and she stares about the chapel, terrified.

"I pronounce you man and wife," says the minister, who is kindly, thin, white-haired. He is very old; in fact he quietly dies the following year.

And then, almost as though nothing had happened, they have all left the chapel: Tom and Barbara, Avery and Devlin, who was Tom's best man. ("I gave my father away" is another of Avery's new post-wedding jokes.) But something has happened: Tom and Barbara are married. They don't believe it either. He gives her a deep and prolonged kiss (why does it look so awkward?) which embarrasses Devlin terribly, so that he stares up and down the pretty tree-lined street. He is thinking of Jessica, who is dead.

And he passionately wishes that she had not died, savagely blames Tom and Barbara for that death. Trivial, entirely selfish people—so he sees them; he compares the frivolity of their connection with Jessica's heavy suffering. Since Jessica's death Devlin has been in a sort of voluntary retreat. He left his window-display job and most of his friends; he stays at home on the wrong side of Telegraph Hill, without a view. He reads a lot and listens to music and does an occasional watercolor. He rarely sees Avery, and disapproves of what he understands to be her life. ("You don't think it's dykey, the way you sleep around?" was the terrible sentence he spoke to her, on the eve of Jessica's funeral, and it has never been retracted.) Sometimes in his fantasies it is ten years back, and Tom and Jessica get a divorce and she comes out to live in San

Francisco. He finds her a pretty apartment on Telegraph Hill and her hair grows beautifully white and she wears nice tweeds and entertains at tea. And Tom and Barbara move to hell—Los Angeles or Mexico or somewhere. Most people who know him assume Devlin to be homosexual; asexual is actually the more accurate description.

They stand there, that quiet striking group, all blinking in a brilliant October sun that instantly dries their tears; for several moments they are all transfixed there, unable to walk to their separate cars, to continue to the friend's house where there is to be the wedding reception. (Why this hesitation? Do none of them believe in the wedding? What is a marriage?)

❧❧

Five years later, in the early Sixties, Avery drives up to Maine from Hilton, for various reasons which do not include a strong desire to see Tom and Barbara. She has been married to Christopher for four years, and she came out from San Francisco to Hilton to see how it was away from him. Away from him she fell wildly in love with a man in Hilton named Jason Valentine, and now (for various reasons) she has decided that she needs some time away from Jason.

She drives smoothly, quietly, along the pine-needled road in her Corvair to find no one there. No car.

But the screen door is unlatched, and she goes in, stepping up from the old stone step onto the long narrow porch, from which the long table has been removed, replaced with a new one that is small and round. (But where did they put the old one?) And there are some bright yellow canvas chairs, new and somehow shocking against the weathered shingled wall. Inside the house are more violent changes, more bright new fabrics: curtains, bandanna-red, and a bandanna bedspread on the conspicuous wide bed. Beside the fireplace is a white wicker sofa (new) with chintz cushions—more red. So much red and so much newness make Avery dizzy; almost angrily she wonders where the old things are, the decaying banners and sepia photographs of girls in Greek costumes. She goes into the kitchen and it is all painted yellow, into what was the large closet where she used to sleep—but a wall has been knocked out between her room and Devlin's; it is all one room now, a new room, entirely strange, with a new iron bed, a crocheted bedspread, which is white. Is that where they will expect her to sleep? She wishes there were a phone. Tomorrow she will have to drive into town to call Jason at his studio.

Needing a drink, Avery goes back into the kitchen, and finds a bottle of an unfamiliar brand of bourbon. She gets ice from the refrigerator (terrifyingly new—so white!), water from the tap—thank God, the same old sink. With her clutched drink she walks quickly through the living room to the porch, down to the end. She looks out across the lake with sentimentally teared eyes, noting that it is clear but not quite clear enough to see Mount Washington.

Being in love with Jason, who is a nonpracticing architect (he would rather paint), who worries about his work (his nonwork), who loves her but is elusive (she has no idea when they will see each other again), has tightened all Avery's nerves: she is taut, cries easily and is all concentrated on being in love with Jason.

A car drives up, a Mustang—Barbara is faithful to Fords. And there they are saying, "Avery, but we didn't *expect* you, we went into *Port*land, for *lob*sters. Oh, dear, how awful, we only bought *two!*" Embracing, laughing. Tears (why?) in everyone's eyes.

They settle down, after packages are put away,

Avery's bags in the new guest room, and they watch the sunset: a disappointing pale pastel. And they drink a lot.

Barbara is nervous, both because of this shift in schedule and because of Avery, whom she regards as an intellectual, like Tom. She is always afraid of what Avery will say—a not unfounded fear. Also, she is upset about the prospect of two lobsters for three people.

What he considers her untimely arrival permits Tom's usual ambivalence about Avery to yield to a single emotion: extreme irritation. How inconsiderate she is—always has been! Besides, he was looking forward to his lobster.

Avery chooses this unpropitious moment to announce that she is leaving Christopher. "We've been making each other miserable," she says. "We have been, for a long time." She trails off.

Tom brightens. "Well, old dear, I always think incompatibility is a good reason not to live together." He has no notion of his own prurience in regard to his daughter.

She does. She says, "Oh, Christ."

Barbara goes into the kitchen to divide up the lobster; a skilled hostess, she does quite well, and she makes a good mayonnaise as she listens to the jagged sounds of the quarrel on the porch. Avery and Tom. She sighs.

Now darkness surrounds the house, and silence, except for a faint soft lapping of small waves on the shore, and tiny noises from the woods: small animals shifting weight on the leaves, a bird moving on a branch.

"Although I have what I suppose is an old-fashioned prejudice against divorce," Tom unfortunately says.

"Christ, is that why you stayed married to mother and made her as miserable as you could? Christ, I have a prejudice against misery!" Avery feels her voice (and herself) getting out of control.

Barbara announces dinner, and they go to the pretty new table, where places are set, candles lit. Barbara distributes the lobster, giving Tom the major share, but he scowls down at his plate.

As Avery does at hers—in Hilton, with Jason, she was generally too overstimulated, too "in love" to eat; now she is exhausted and very hungry. She turns to Barbara, as though for help. "Don't you ever wish you'd got married before you did? What a waste those years were. That time in San Francisco, why not then?"

Startled, Barbara has no idea what to answer. She has never allowed herself to think in these terms, imaginatively to revise her life. "I feel lucky we've had these years we have had," she says—which, for her, is the truth. She loves Tom; she feels that she is lucky to be his wife.

"But those last years were horrible for Mother," Avery says. "You might have spared her that time."

"I think I might be in a better position than you to be the judge of that." Enraged, Tom takes a characteristic stance: his chin thrust out, he is everyone's superior— he is especially superior to women and children, particularly his own.

"Oh, yeah?" In her childhood, this was considered the rudest remark one could make; then Avery would never have said it to Tom. "You think she just plain died of a heart attack, don't you? Well, her room was full of empty sherry bottles. All over. Everywhere those drab brown empty bottles, smelling sweet. Julia told me, when she cleaned it out."

This information (which is new) is so shocking (and so absolutely credible) to Tom that he must dismiss it at once. His desperate and hopeless guilts toward Jessica have forced him to take a sanctimonious tone in speaking of her. He must dismiss this charge at once.

"As a matter of fact, Julia is quite unreliable, as Verlie was," he says.

Avery explodes. "Julia is unreliable! Verlie was! Christ—why? Because they're black? Because they're women?"

Barbara has begun to cry. "You've got to stop this," she says. "Why quarrel about the past? It's over—"

Tom and Avery stare at each other, in terrible pain; they would like to weep, to embrace, but they are unable to do either.

Tom draws himself up stiffly—stiffly he turns to Barbara. "You're quite right, old dear," he says.

Several things attack Avery's mind at once: one, that she would like to say goddam you both, or something obscene, and take off down the turnpike, back to Boston; two, she is too drunk for the turnpike; and three, she has just noticed that Tom speaks to Barbara exactly as though she were Jessica, as though neither of them were a person but something generic named Wife.

And so the moment goes, the awful emotions subside and they all retreat to trivia. Although Avery's hands still shake, she comments on the mayonnaise (she is not excruciatingly Southern Jessica's daughter for nothing), which Barbara gratefully takes up.

"I'm never sure it will come out right," she says. "I've had the most embarrassing failures, but of course tonight, just for family—" She is unable to finish the sentence, or to remember what she meant.

Later, during the next few years before Tom's death, Avery looks back and thinks that yes, she should have left then, drunk or not. She could have found a motel. That would have been a strong gesture, a refusal to put up with any more of what she saw as Tom's male imperialism, his vast selfishness. (But poor Avery was constantly plagued with alternatives; she constantly rewrote her life into new versions in which she did not marry Stanley. Or Christopher. After Tom died she thought that perhaps it was just as well she hadn't left, but she was never quite sure.

❧

Against everyone's advice, early in the summer after Tom died, Barbara drove alone to Maine. Even Devlin had called to dissuade her. (In fact ever since Tom's funeral, to which Avery did not even come—Tom had died while she was in Mount Zion Hospital being treated for depression—a new and warm connection had been established between Barbara and Devlin; they wrote back and forth; she phoned him for various pieces of advice—she had begun to rely on him as she was used to relying on Tom.)

Devlin said, "Darling Barbara, do you see it as an exercise in masochism? I wouldn't have thought it of you."

"Angel, you don't understand. I love that house. I've been extremely happy there."

"Barbara, let me be blunt: don't you think you'll be fantastically lonely?"

"No, I don't."

And so, after visits with friends and relatives in Boston, Barbara drives on to Maine in her newest Ford, and arrives in a twilight of early July. She parks near the house, gets out, pausing only briefly to observe the weather, which is clear, and to smile at the warm familiar smell of pines. Then she walks briskly over to the porch and opens the padlock on the screen door.

Her first reaction, stepping up onto the porch, could be considered odd: she decides that those yellow chairs are wrong for the porch. This pleases her: changing them for something else will give her something to do. She enters the living room, sniffs at the musty, airless space and goes into the kitchen, where last summer she

51

hid a bottle of bourbon in the flour bin. (Sometimes stray hunters or fishermen break into the house and take things.) No one has taken it, and she makes herself a good stiff drink, and goes to the rounded end of the porch, to sit and rest.

And much more clearly than she can remember anything that happened last month, last winter or fall, she sees that scene of over thirty years ago, sees Tom (how young he was, how handsome) as he urged her to play her ukulele (play what? did he name a song?), and she sees Jessica come out to where they are (making some reference to the girls who used to come to camp—poor Jessica), and Wilfred, as always angrily serious, puffing although not yet fat, and then wild, skinny Avery (why did she and Jason Valentine not marry?) and frightened Devlin, holding his mother's arm. She sees all those people, and herself among them, and for an instant she has a sense that she *is* all of them—that she is Jessica as well as Barbara, is Wilfred, Avery, Devlin and Tom.

But this is an unfamiliar mood, or sense, for her, and she shakes it off, literally shaking her head and lifting her chin. She remembers then that she put the old chairs and the table in the shed next to the kitchen.

Three days later Barbara has restored the lodge to what (to herself) she calls its "old look." The old chairs and old table are back. She has even put up some of Jessica's old pictures in the living room.

She has no idea why she made such an effort, except that she firmly believes (always has) in the efficacy of physical work; she was driven by a strong, controlling instinct, and she also believes in her instincts. She even laughs to herself at what could seem a whim, and in writing a note to Devlin she says, "You'd have thought I was restoring Williamsburg, and you should see my blisters!"

And so at the end of her day she is seated there at the

end of the porch, and everything but herself looks just as it did when she first saw it. She drinks the two stiff highballs that she allows herself before dinner, and she remembers all the best times with Tom, San Francisco hotels and Paris honeymoon, the big parties in Hilton, and she sheds a few tears, but she does not try to change anything that happened. She does not imagine an altered, better life that she might have had.

Winter Rain

Whenever in the final unendurable weeks of winter, I am stricken, as now, to the bone with cold—it is raining, the furnace has somehow failed—I remember that winter of 1947–1948 in Paris, when I was colder than ever in my life, when it always rained, when everything broke down. That was the winter of strikes: GRÈVE GÉNÉRALE, in large strange headlines. And everyone struck: Métro, garbage, water, electricity, mail—all these daily necessities were at one time or another with difficulty forgone. Also, that was the first winter of American students—boys on the G.I. bill and girls with money from home, Bennington meeting Princeton in the Montana Bar. There were cellar clubs to which French friends guided one mysteriously: on the Rue Dauphine the Tabu, with a band; the Mephisto, just off the Boulevard Saint-Germain; and further out on Rue Blomet the wicked Bal Nègre, where one danced all night to West Indian music, danced with everyone and drank Pernod. It was a crowded, wild, excited year.

I think of friends of that time—I have kept up with none of them, certainly not with Bruno, nor Laura, nor Joe, not even with Mme. Frenaye. And it gloomily occurs to me that they may all be dead, Bruno in some violent Italian way, Laura and Joe in Hollywood, and Mme. Frenaye of sheer old age, on the Rue de Courcelles, *"tout près,"* as she used to say, *"du Parc Monceau."* Though we parted less than friends, it is she of whom I think most often.

Madame and I really parted, as from the first I should have known we would, over money. And, more than I regret the loss of our connection, I regret the sordidness of its demise. But I should have known; the process was gradual but clear. As was the fact that I, and not she, would lose face in any conflict.

⚜

To begin with, she extracted from me an enormous amount of money for permission to live at the cold end of the long drafty hall in her flat. Of course I didn't have to take the room, or to accept the arrangement at all, but from the first I was seduced. I had heard, from friends, that a Mme. Frenaye might be willing to take a nice American girl student into her charming home. I inquired further, and was invited to tea. It was raining dreadfully, even in September, and I wore, all wet and shivering, a yellow summer coat and summer dress since, probably owing to a strike somewhere, my trunk of winter clothes had not arrived. The street seemed impossibly gray, chilled and forbidding, but the central room of the flat into which I was ushered by Madame was warm and graceful. There were exquisite white Louis XVI chairs, a marvelous muted blue Persian rug, a mantel lined with marble above a fireplace in which a small fire blazed prettily.

Mme. Frenaye was a great goddess of a woman. She must have been sixty, or even seventy—I was never sure—but she was very tall and she held herself high; she was Junoesque indeed. She still mourned her

55

husband, dead five years, and wore only black, but her effect was vivid. Her hair was bright gold and she wore it in a thick crowning braid across the waves that rose from her brow. Her eyes were very blue, capable of a great spectacle of innocence or charming guile, and she wore mascara heavily on her long lashes. She had dimples and perfect white teeth.

❧❦❧

We took tea from a beautiful table before the fire, and we talked about Antibes, where I had spent the summer. Mme. Frenaye poured a little rum from a pretty porcelain jug into the tea, and said, "I would not have thought of going to the Riviera in the summer. So crowded then. But of course you are so young, you have not been to France before."

She seemed prepared to forgive, and I did not want to protest that I had had a very good time.

She went on, "But a winter in Paris, there you have chosen wisely, this time you will not regret your choice. Theatre, opera, it is all here for you, the best in the world. And of course the Sorbonne, since you have chosen to study." She was vastly amused to learn that the name of my course at the Sorbonne was *Cours de la civilisation française.* "But you will spend the rest of your life—" she said, and I agreed.

We talked, and drank our tea, and ate small delicious cakes, until it occurred to me that I had perhaps stayed too long and so rose to leave. I think I had really forgotten that I had come about a room, or perhaps such a crass consideration seemed inappropriate in Louis XVI surroundings. Instead, on the way out I admired a painting. Mme. Frenaye said, "Ah, yes, and it has a gross value." I translate literally to give the precise effect of her words on me. My French was not good, and I thought I had misheard her, or not known an idiom. I would not be warned.

Then, at the door, while helping me with my still damp yellow coat, she said that she had heard that I needed a pleasant place to live, that she would be willing to let me live there, that she would serve me breakfast and dinner, and she named an outrageous number of francs. Even translated into dollars it was high. I was so stunned by her whole method that I accepted on the spot, and it was agreed that I would bring my things on the following Monday. That I did not even ask to see the room is evidence of my stupor; I must have thought it would be exactly like the salon.

And sometimes now I wonder whether she had any idea that I would accept; or made up that ridiculous figure simply to let me off. And I wonder too if I did not want to prove that I could do better than yellow coats and summer dresses in a cold September rain; behind me there were sound American dollars, and, as my father would have said, more where they came from. So, from our combined dubious motives, we were joined, to live and eat and talk together throughout those difficult historic months from September until February, until our private war became visible and manifest, and I left.

❧

The room was actually not as bad as it might have been, taken on such dazzled faith. It was not large, nor warm, nor did it contain a desk or a bookcase; however, the bed was regally gilded and huge and soft, and I slept under comforting layers of down, between pink linen sheets. Madame sighed, her beautiful eyes misted as she showed the bed to me and I felt badly about so depriving her until I realized that her own small bed-sitting room had been astutely chosen as the warmest room in the house. And the grand bed would not fit into it.

❦

When I said such things to Laura and Joe, later to Bruno, as we hunched over beers in the steamy Café de Flore or the Deux Magots, they reasonably exclaimed, "But why on earth do you stay there?" (Laura and Joe were Marxists, and I was acceptable to them partly because my arrangement with Mme. Frenaye left me with virtually no money at all.) In any case I did not think that they would feel the charm of Mme. Frenaye, and so I would say to them, "But the food is fantastic, and see how my French is improving."

Both of these things were quite true. I have never since tasted anything to compare with her *poisson normand,* that beautifully flaking fat white fish baked with tiny mushrooms, tiny shrimps and mussels in white wine. I have the most vivid sensual memories of her crisp green salads. I would arrive cold and usually wet from my long Métro trek, and hurriedly unwrap myself from my coat just in time to enter that small warm room where she had placed the white-clothed table. The room was full of marvelous delicate smells of hot food, and Madame in passage from the kitchen would greet me. *"Bon soir, Patience. Mais vous avez froid. Asseyez-vous, je viens tout de suite. Oh, mais j' ai oublié l'essentiel—"* and she was off to fetch the decanter of wine.

And my French did improve. She knew no English, and we talked animatedly throughout those months of dinners. She was endlessly curious about America, though she pretended to disbelieve half of what I told her. "But, Patience, surely you exaggerate," she would

58

chide, in a tone of amused tolerance. Sometimes, fresh from Joe's lectures, I became heavily sociological. She listened intently, nodded appropriately. Only when I hit on American anti-Semitism did I strike some chord in her—she found it absolutely incomprehensible. She adored American Jews. Her husband had been a cotton merchant, and in his business the only Americans he met were Jewish or from Texas. And the Texans, according to Madame, were appalling: they ordered the most expensive champagne or cognac and then got drunk on it. The Jewish families whom she met were quite another story. *"Tellement cultivées, tellement sensibles."* Her most admired American friends, the Berkowitzes *("Ah, les Berkowitz")*, went to museums daily, to the theatre and the opera; the Texans never. She felt that *"les Berkowitz"* too squandered their money but in less visible and offensive ways. One of her most loved stories was of going shopping for a brassière, a *soutien-gorge,* with Marion Berkowitz. *"C'était tout, tout petit,"* she would say, with her thumb and forefinger gesturing a pinch of nothing, *"et ça coûtait tellement cher!"* This contradiction never ceased to amaze and delight her.

The truth was that I liked Mme. Frenaye. I admired her beauty and her charm; and her scorn, her assumption of superiority to the world, comforted me since I felt that she counted me on her side. Moreover, I simply could not imagine a scene in which I told her that I was going to leave. I think that if I had not met Bruno, near Christmas, during one long night in the Bal Nègre, where I had reluctantly gone with Laura and Joe, I would have lived on the Rue de Courcelles until June, when I took that huge and final boat for New York.

My memory of Bruno is also involved with the cold: I see the two of us clinging together in a garish white-lit Métro entrance, because it was too cold outside, and our partings were endless and all unendurable. We walked together. I remember my ungloved hand pressing against his, together jammed deeply into his shabby tweed pocket, as we walked past steamed bright windows in the iron cold, stopping to kiss.

Even Bruno seems legendary to me now; both our romantic intensity and the facts of his life sound mythic. His father was an Italian anti-Fascist who had left Italy in the Twenties. Bruno was born in Toulouse, and spent his fifteenth birthday in a Vichy concentration camp, his sixteenth in a similar camp in Italy. He had fought with the Maquis, and with guerrilla fighters in the Italian Alps. He had no scars nor any limp to show for all of this; he was tall and sturdy, smooth-skinned, clear-eyed as any innocent American boy—in fact he was often taken for a G.I., which amused him and privately annoyed me. He studied law in Paris, and lived with relatives out in the 14th arrondissement. Thus in the cold we had no place to go, and between partings we dreamed of a furnished room, warm and light, anywhere in Paris. I can no longer remember the substance of our quarrels, nor of our talk, but both went on forever, punctuating each other, and all the time our eyes held together, our hands touched.

Out of some misguided sense of duty I spent Christmas Day that year with Madame rather than with Bruno. And it was a bad day. Madame was far from being at her best. She sniffed deprecatingly at my gift of a tiny bottle of perfume from Worth, telling me she had once calculated the contents of all the bottles on her dressing table and it came to more than two liters. "You can imagine," she said, "how much that would be worth." She had given me a pair of felt slippers from Trois Quartiers, and they were not very pretty.

We rallied somewhat at dinner. There was an incredible roast chicken, an unheard-of luxury in Paris that year. But then, with the token glass of brandy, Mme. Frenaye grew sad again, and spoke of the death of her husband. "Over and over he said to me, 'Ah, how good you are,'" and her great eyes misted. I was wildly impatient to go; I had promised to meet Bruno at the Flore at nine. I wanted to hear of no other love, no death.

That night we fought because I lived so far away. Bruno found incomprehensible my refusal to move. "On purpose you isolate yourself in your gray prison," he said. (Once he had accompanied me home, had seen from the outside the fortress of apartments on the Rue de Courcelles.) He said, his clear blue eyes near mine, "How much more time we would have if you even lived near the Sorbonne—I think you don't want to be with me—you would rather stay safely beside your little fire." I protested this violently, but in a sense it was perfectly true. I was afraid of him; life with Madame, though difficult, seemed safer than the exposure of a room alone.

But at the same time that I resisted Bruno I found my fortress more and more impossible. I was extremely tense; the most petty annoyances grew large. I once calculated that with all the small sums of money which Madame had borrowed from time to time to tip porters, buy stamps, I could have bought Bruno a gaudy present.

And there was the matter of my CARE packages. My anxious mother sent them punctually each month, thus assuring herself that I would never starve. I had written and asked her not to. Their arrival embarrassed me; I was sure the porter who carried them upstairs knew what they were, and thought of his own hungry family. I wanted badly to give them to him, but some misplaced shyness held me back. Madame adored all that American food. She appropriated each package and opened it on the marble-topped kitchen table. She exclaimed over, and later used, the boxes of cake mix, and she devised a marvelous method of stuffing baked potatoes with the liver pâté that came in large cans. The pancake mix she especially loved. *"Ah, les crêpes américaines,"* she would cry out lovingly, expressing her whole indulgent fondness for the young rich crazy country of dollars and handsome brave G.I.s, of fantastic machines that did everything, of her cherished Berkowitzes and of me.

But in my new mood of sullen resentment I protested her appropriation. How dare she charge me ruinous rates for food and lodging and then accept such a bulk of food from my mother? In silence and secrecy my list of grievances against her mounted; that they were petty and degrading of course made them more unbearable. Also that I lacked the courage to say anything.

It was perfectly appropriate to that year that my dilemma was finally resolved by a strike. And by Bruno.

❧❦❧

All during January, Bruno snarled and complained at my living arrangements. I remember an afternoon in the upstairs part of the Flore, where it was always warm and with luck one could stay for hours, seated on the plaid-covered banquettes, without having to order anything. We had, I remember, not enough money between us for hot chocolate—which we both felt could have saved the afternoon. Unkindly, Bruno reminded me that if I lived in the Quarter, in a cheap room, I could now be making hot chocolate and serving it in privacy. There was always a sort of European practicality about him—even in love, I thought—and in the phrase betrayed how American was my own romanti-

62

cism. He gave a sense of the pressure of time, of destiny, as though along his way he could not be troubled with incidents of geography and money. By the end of the afternoon we had agreed never to meet again, and I wept conspicuously all the long Métro ride from Odéon to Place Péreire.

❦

The next week was unendurable. There was a violent cold black rain. The heat failed again in Madame's long flat, the fires spluttered and would not burn. Wholly miserable, I mourned my forever lost love.

Then came the mail strike. No letters at all, from anywhere. The papers described mountains of paper piled fantastically on post-office floors. I was completely dependent on letters from home for money, and now I could not pay Madame on the day when my fee came due. At dinner I tried to mention it casually to her. Much in the spirit of the times, I said, "After all, this strike can't go on forever."

But Madame's spirit was not at all with the times. "Strike or not, I have to shop for groceries," she said with uncharacteristic terseness. I was totally upset; life, I felt, was too much for me; I had no resources. And even Madame, stronger and wiser and infinitely more charming, fell down. Apropos of nothing she told me again the story of Marion Berkowitz and the buying of the *soutien-gorge,* but the mention of high prices made us both nervous and we failed to be amused.

That night, hunched frozen between the pink linen sheets, I decided that if I did not see Bruno again I would die.

At breakfast my final long-delayed scene with Mme. Frenaye took place, over cups of powdered American coffee from my latest CARE package. I found that I had to say everything all at once. "I have to move," I said.

63

"It's very nice here but I simply can't afford it any longer. And really, you know, no one pays so much for a pension, I mean even in America this would be considered high. And also this is too far from my classes at the Sorbonne—you remember during the Métro strike I couldn't even get there."

Madame listened to this somewhat with the air of a teacher of speech. And indeed it was a tribute to the French I had learned with her that I was able to get it out. She seemed, on the whole, to approve both my eloquence and my logic, for at the end she said, *"Certainement,"* in a final tone.

I needed her to argue with me, and I added defiantly, "I want to live in the Latin Quarter."

"Oui, le Quartier Latin." But she was not thinking about my proposed life on the Left Bank; her tone was completely neutral. And hearing it I realized suddenly that as far as she was concerned I had already gone. Also, and this was doubly infuriating, I realized that she had undoubtedly known for some time that I would go. Probably from that first wet day when we took our tea by her pretty fire she had known that I would not last the year. Any concession on her part—if she had said she could wait for the rent—might have made me weaken. But she was far too realistic and too economical for any emotional waste.

❧

And so I packed that afternoon in a fury of frustration. I felt that I had been taken, conned out of my moment of righteous defiance by some ageless European trick of charm. As I hunted for shoe bags, I thought furiously that she had completely turned the tables. I was the one who had ended by being mercenary, petty.

She came to the door later, and asked perfunctorily if there was anything that she could do to help, and I

64

wanted to shout "No!" at her, but I did not; I only muttered negatively. She said, "Well, in that case I will say *au revoir, Patience, et bonne chance.*"

We shook hands at the door to my erstwhile bedroom, and I said that I would call her when I was settled, and she said, "But please do," and smiled with her beautiful wise blue eyes and was gone. I had no true parting scene.

The room that I found late that afternoon was on the Rue de Seine. My high narrow windows overlooked the entrance to the Club Mephisto; I could see a fish market where the fat silver bellies were piled high, and a fruit stand bright with winter tomatoes and bunches of dark rose chrysanthemums. At the corner hardware store I bought a saucepan and a small tripod burner with some cans of Sterno, and felt myself prepared for warm domestic peace with Bruno.

❦

But though reunited we were never peaceful. In spite of my room, of which he approved, our passionate partings continued. I can hear now the angry sound of his boots on the narrow steep stairs as he left stormily after an impossible argument. And I remember lying half awake dreaming that he would come back.

One afternoon, during a rift with Bruno that was more prolonged than usual, on an impulse I called Mme. Frenaye and asked her to have tea with me at the Ritz. She would be delighted, she said, and I remember that I wore my first New Look dress, which was gray silk with a terribly long skirt. The occasion was a great success. I was struck by how glad I was to see her. It seemed to me then that I had missed her, and that my life alone had been more difficult. Certainly that afternoon Madame was at her best. She complained pleasantly that the service was not what it had been before the war, nor the pastry, and after our tea we gossiped happily about the other women in the room.

Madame did not ask me about my present living arrangements. Since I had come prepared to boast, this was slightly irritating, but at the same time I was relieved. Nor did she, as I had rather expected, say that she missed me. She was quite impersonally charming, and we parted with an exchange of pleasantries, but with no talk of a further meeting.

The rain and cold continued into April. I remember bitterly deciding that the lyric burst one expected of spring in Paris would never come, that it was a myth.

Joe and Laura had left, apologizing, for Hollywood in March. I went to lectures at the Sorbonne and in the lengthening intervals when I did not see Bruno I wandered alone about the city, hunched against the rain, wrapped in American tweed.

Then, around the first of May, the weather changed, the chestnut and plane trees along the boulevards feathered into delicate green and the sky behind the square stone tower of Saint-Germain-des-Prés was pink and soft in the long light evenings.

For at least a month Bruno and I got along happily. It was the tender penultimate stage of a love affair, before it became clear that I really wanted him to come to America and marry me, and that he had to live in Italy and did not want to get married, clear to us both that I was hopelessly domestic and bourgeois. He said, finally, that I would not be a suitable companion for an Italian statesman, and of course he was perfectly right.

But before this finality, in some spirit of bravado, I called Mme. Frenaye and asked her to come to tea in my room—and asked Bruno to come too. I am not at all sure what I expected of either of them; perhaps I felt the dramatic necessity of a meeting between the two people who had that year been, variously, most important to me.

Or perhaps this was my last defiance of Madame. If that were so I failed utterly, foiled again by her aplomb. Of course Bruno helped; he appeared uncharacteristically in a white shirt and tie, his brown hair brushed smooth; he could not have looked less like an Italian radical with a violent past. Mme. Frenaye first took him to be a nice American boy; her whole demeanor spoke a total acceptance and approval of him. She thought it very wise of him to study law in Paris, and she raised her lovely innocent blue eyes in attractive horror when he told her how many hours he had to study each day. "But then you are so young and strong," she said, with a tender and admiring smile. Of course he liked her—who could not?

❧

She even approved of my room, though she sat rather stiffly and gingerly on the single straight wooden chair. She looked across the street to the piles of fish and remarked that she had noticed lower prices here than in her own *quartier,* but this was her only suggestion that I had come down in the world. And I thought then, but did not speak, of her beautiful *poisson normand.* She only said, "Such a nice clean room, Patience, and it must be so convenient for you."

I made tea, boiling the water over Sterno which Madame thought terribly ingenious, and we ate the pastries which I had bought. Bruno and Madame talked about the beauties of Italy, of Florence in early spring, Venice in October. And painting. I could imagine her saying of him, *"Tellement cultivé, ce jeune Italien, tellement sensible."*

After that day everything deteriorated. The weather turned cold and it rained fiercely as though to remind us all of the difficult past winter. When, finally, I booked passage on a boat which was to leave the third of June,

I felt that my exit was being forced, the city and the time would have no more of me. I had accepted the impossibility of Bruno—we still saw each other but I wept and it always ended badly. I did not see Madame again. I did call her, meaning to say goodbye, but there was no answer.

Sometimes it occurs to me to write to Madame, to send her pictures of my husband, my house and my children, as though to convince her that I have grown up, that I am no longer that odd girl who came to her in the wet summer coat, or who tried to charm her with tea made over Sterno in an unlikely room. Or I try to imagine her here, perhaps as the great-aunt whom, on shopping trips into town, I occasionally visit. But this is impossible: my aunt, an American Gothic puritan with a band of black grosgrain ribbon about her throat, my aunt laughing over the purchase of a tiny *soutien-gorge*, bringing in wine, *l'essentiel?* This won't do. And I am forced to leave Madame, and Bruno of whom I never think, as and where they are, in that year of my own history.

Gift of Grass

"But what's so great about money—or marriages and houses, for that matter?" Strengthened perhaps by two recent cups of tea (rose hips, brewed with honey and a few grass seeds), Cathy had raised herself on one elbow and turned to face the doctor. "Couldn't there be other ways to live?" she asked, consciously childish and pleading.

"Have you thought of one?" Oppressed by weariness and annoyance, Dr. Fredericks was unaware that both those emotions sounded in his soft, controlled voice. Once, in a burst of confidence, Cathy had said to him accusingly, "You speak so softly just to make me listen." Now she said nothing. Believing himself to be in command, Dr. Fredericks also believed his patient to be overcome by what he saw as her transference. She saw her feelings toward him as simple dislike and a more complicated distrust.

She lay back down, giving up, and reconsidered the large space that served as both the doctor's office and his living room. It was coolly blue and green—olive walls and ceiling, royal-blue carpet, navy silk chair and sofa, pale-blue linen lampshades on green pottery lamps. Only the couch on which Cathy lay was neither green nor blue; it was upholstered with a worn Oriental rug, as though that might disguise its function. Like most children—she was sixteen—Cathy knew more than her elders thought she did. She knew that at one time her mother had been a patient of Dr. Frederick's, and she recognized her mother's touch in that room. Her mother, who was an interior decorator, had evidently "done" it. As payment for her hours of lying there? It would have been an expensive job; Cathy saw that, too. God knows how many hours it would have taken to pay for all that silk.

All her mother had ever said, in a tearful voice that was supposed to extract similar sincerity from Cathy, was "At one time in my life when I was very troubled, a psychiatrist really helped me a great deal. In fact, you might say that he saved our marriage, Bill's and mine." Not wanting Cathy to sense a conspiracy, she had not told Cathy that she was sending her to her own psychiatrist. This was in August, when Cathy had said that she was not going back to school in the fall, and her mother and Bill—her stepfather for the past ten years—had told her that in that case she must go to see Dr. Fredericks.

"But I'm not troubled," Cathy had lied. Then she had giggled in her unrelated, unnerving way. "Or married. I just don't want to go to school for a while," she had said.

"But I hope you will be married," her mother had said. She had sighed, frowned and then smiled, attempting reassurance. "Dr. James helped me a great deal," she said. "He's one of the best doctors in San Francisco." She used the first name of Dr. Fredericks—Dr. James Fredericks—which Cathy did not think was a very smart disguise.

While the long pause after his question lasted, Dr. Fredericks struggled with his counter-transference. He stared down at Cathy's rather squat, short body in its jeans and black turtleneck sweater, at the long, limp brown hair that fell from the edge of the couch and the perfectly round brown eyes in a pale, round face. He had to admit it—he couldn't stand the little girl. Injecting kindliness into his voice, he said, "Isn't there anything on your mind that you'd like to tell me about?"

At this, Cathy burst into tears. A quick, noisy storm of sobs shook her shoulders and her chest, then stopped, and she said, "You dumb fink."

He leaned back comfortably in his raw-silk chair that did not creak. Seductively he said, "I suppose by your standards I am in some ways rather dumb." He did not say, Such as they are.

"Such as they are," she said. "I'm not interested in standards, or school or earning money or getting married."

"I wish I knew what you were interested in," he said.

This seemed to Cathy his most heartfelt and least contrived remark of the hour, and she answered him. "Clouds," she said. "And foghorns. I wonder where they all are."

"If you really wonder, you could go to the library and get a book."

"I'd rather wonder." She giggled.

"The 'trip' is more important than the destination, is that what you mean?" Despite himself, he had underlined "trip."

"I don't drop acid, I've told you that," she said, deadpan.

"Well," he said, warming to his task, "that's a reasonable enough fear. But perhaps you have some other less reasonable fears."

"Deer-hunters. God, they have the worst faces I ever saw," she suddenly brought out, forgetting him and remembering the weekend just past. She and her mother and Bill had driven up to Lake Tahoe—a jaunt intended to prove that they were not really angry with Cathy, that they loved her nevertheless. By an unfortunate coincidence, this was also the first weekend of the deer season. On the other side of Sacramento, winding up past Auburn through beautiful mountain rocks and trees, Highway 80 had been lined with white camper trucks bearing hunters. The men wore ugly red caps and red plaid shirts. They had looked remarkably alike, at least to Cathy—as alike as their campers. Fathers and sons and friends, their faces had been coarse and unintelligent, excited, jovial and greedy. "God, I hope they all shoot each other," she said to Dr. Fredericks.

"Well," he said hopefully. "Let's see if we can find out what deer-hunters mean to you. I doubt somehow that it's sheer dislike of killing. For instance, you don't seem to be upset about the war in Vietnam."

"That's so bad I can't think about it at all," said Cathy, with total candor.

"Well, let's see," Dr. Fredericks, almost alone among his colleagues, was more opposed to protesters than to the war, but bringing up Vietnam had been a ploy. He now thrust his real point home. "I do seem to remember that your stepfather is something of a hunter," he said.

Cathy heard the light note of triumph in his voice, to which she reacted with rage and despair and a prolonged silence. Why bother to tell him that Bill only hunted ducks—and only with his father, before that awful old man had died? During the silence, she listened to the leisurely sounds of outlying San Francisco traffic and the faint, distant foghorns from the Bay. Concentrating on these, she was able to stop the echo of Dr. Frederick's voice in her mind. Their voices were what she could stand least about adults: Dr. Frederick's bored hostility; her teachers' voices, loud and smug; the alternately anxious and preening, knowing voice of her mother. The only thing that she could remember about her natural father, who had divorced her mother when Cathy was two, was his voice. It was high-pitched, almost a whine—nothing much to miss. Actually, Bill had a nice warm deep voice, until he drank too much and it blurred.

A heavy truck went by, creaking and lumbering as though weighted with old furniture or barrels of china and glass. Brakes screeched several blocks away. Then the traffic sounds continued as before. For a few minutes there were no foghorns, and then there they were again, discordant, with no rhythm.

Both Cathy and Dr. Fredericks glanced over at the clock on his desk. Five minutes to go. He sighed softly and pleasurably. He had recently stopped smoking and he enjoyed the air in his expanded lungs. Although he was nearing sixty, he was well preserved. Squash and swimming at his club had kept him in shape; he felt a certain snobbery toward many of his colleagues who were running to fat. He and his wife, who owned and ran an extremely successful chain of gift shops, spent vacations at health spas, playing tennis and dieting together. A blue-eyed Southerner, from West Virginia, Dr. Fredericks liked to view himself as a maverick among psychoanalysts—another breed, one might say.

Cathy swung her short legs off the couch and sat up. She clutched her knees and faced him. "Look," she said. "It's hopeless. You and Mother think it's impor-tant to get married and save marriages and get money and save that, and I don't."

"We're trying to find out what you do think is important," he said. He did not bother to conceal his impatience.

Neither did she. "So am I."

"Next week?" They both stood up.

Out of context (he felt), she giggled.

Cathy's parents lived about ten blocks from Dr. Fredericks in the same expensive and fog-ridden San Francisco neighborhood, but instead of going home Cathy walked to the park she often went to, along the broad streets and down the hill leading toward the Bay. Here the sun was shining. She pulled a small box of raisins from her pocket and began to eat them as she walked.

The park was surrounded by rolling woods of pine and fir, cypress and eucalyptus, through which on clear days one could catch blue views of the Bay, red glimpses of the Golden Gate Bridge. Cathy walked past creaking swings and a slide crowded with small children. Out on a playing field, lounging about on the beaten grass, there were some kids her own age whom she thought she knew, so she hurried on toward the woods.

Off the path, she came to a place where there was a large sloping patch of sand. She sat down and reached into the back pocket of her jeans, where there was a very mashed joint, which she lit. She lay back, her left arm protecting her hair from the sand. She sucked in and waited for the melting of her despair.

The air smelled of the sea, of lemon-scented eucalyptus, of pine and of the dank, dark earth. It was nearly a clear day, but the foghorns sounded more strongly to her from the water. Soon the fog would come in, gigantically billowing through the Golden Gate. Now, in the visible sky above the dark thatched cypresses, there were only a few large clouds; they were as heavy and slow and lumbering as bulls, a slow-motion lumbering of bulls across the sky. Cathy concentrated on their changes, their slow and formal shifts in shape and pattern. Then, in the peace, in the warm silence, she fell asleep.

Bill, Cathy's stepfather, had at moments a few of the reactions to Cathy that she evoked in Dr. Fredericks. At worst, he despaired of ever reaching her. But he was exceptionally sensitive to the feelings of women. He could often feel what Cathy felt, and could bear it no better than she. It was his sensitivity, in fact, that had kept him from leaving Cathy's mother, Barbara, who was his second wife. The extent of Barbara's anxiety and despair when they first spoke of separation had got through to him. They had seen Dr. Fredericks, together and separately, for more than a year. But before their meetings with him began Bill had already decided not, after all, to leave Barbara for Ruth, his girl friend. (Ruth had been unhappy, too, but she was younger and more resilient; her despair hit Bill with lesser force.)

Perhaps to avoid a discussion of Ruth, Bill had talked about his inheritance from his father, and Dr. Fredericks had given Bill good advice about investing it. Bill gave him credit for that. Actually investments were Frederick's real but unacknowledged field of expertise. Bill was a commercial artist, and not a terribly successful one. The investment had brought his income well within range of his wife's, so it may have been Dr. Fredericks, after all, who saved the marriage.

It was nearly dinnertime when Cathy came home from the park, and Bill and her mother were sitting in the living room having drinks. Barbara had done their living room, like Dr. Fredericks's, in cool blues and greens, except for the brown leather sofa—a kind of tribute to Bill's masculine presence; ordinarily, she did not use leather. Bill almost never sat on it. He would sit instead, as he did now, on a small Victorian dark-blue silk chair that must have been intended for Cathy. Fortunatly, he was light—a very thin, narrowly built man with delicate bones and sparse blondish hair. Barbara, wearing a smart gray wool dress, was sitting on the leather sofa, and Cathy joined her there. During

75

the cocktail hour, they would sit that way, at opposite ends of the sofa, facing Bill rather than each other.

Mother and daughter appeared to Bill remarkably alike. Barbara's eyes, too, were round and often opaque; her body tended to be squat. Its shape was childlike, which at times Bill found quite touching. At other times, it turned him off, and on to voluptuous Ruth. In Cathy, naturally enough, the sexlessness was more marked. Bill sometimes wondered how he would have felt with a voluptuous daughter, a swinging chick. Would it have made him more uncomfortable?

"I told Dr. Fredericks how much I hated deer-hunters," proffered Cathy. Since Barbara, on principle, would never ask what went on during "her hour," Cathy would throw out indecipherable and tantalizing tidbits.

Feeling his second drink, Bill said, "God, I hate them too. They all remind me of my father." Bill's father had been a mighty hunter, out of the great Northwest, with rather Bunyanesque notions of manhood, so that Bill had trouble from time to time believing in himself as a man, feeling that if those coarse, red-faced, hunting cretins were men he was not one. Indeed, he had been told by several women, including Barbara, that he played around only in order to prove his manhood to himself. At times, he thought that might be true. At other times, he thought it was simply because he very much liked women, lots of them.

But he was not supposed to voice as strong an emotion as hatred in the presence of Cathy, and he sensed reproof in Barbara's slightly stiffened posture. She was an extremely nice woman who wanted things to be perfect—her house, her husband, her daughter and especially herself. Now, instead of reproving Bill, she smiled at him, sighed and said, "God, I'm tired. I really did have a day."

"You didn't like your father?" Cathy asked in a neutral voice that bore, for Bill, an unnerving resemblance to Dr. Fredericks's therapeutic blandness. But it was almost the first personal question that he could remember Cathy's ever asking him, and he found that his chest warmed and expanded with pleasure. "To tell you the truth," he said, "I was very much afraid of him. The way I find hunters frightening."

"Oh," said Cathy, and then for no reason she giggled.

"We're having a really wicked dinner," Barbara said. "Prawns with that sour-cream sauce. I absolutely couldn't resist them in the Grant Market, so big and perfect. And, of course, rice."

"You *are* wicked," Bill responded, since this was how they talked to each other, but he was hearing them both with Cathy's ears, and he wondered how she could bear their middle-aged fatuity. She was staring at a small porcelain vase of tiny blue strawflowers as though she had never seen it before. Bill asked Barbara if she wanted another drink.

He made them strong, and by the end of dinner, during which he and Barbara drank wine and told Cathy illuminating vignettes from their own histories, stressing education and travel and friendship, reminding her that they had once been young—by the time all that was over, Bill was almost drunk and Barbara had a headache. But he was still aware of the troubled depths of tenderness in Barbara's round brown eyes as she said good night to them both—quite out of character, she had decided to give in to her headache and go to bed.

"Cathy and I will clear up," said Bill decisively.

The truth was that he liked to wash dishes, which his father had seen to it that he was not allowed to do. He liked all that warm, foamy water around his hands and the essential and marvelous simplicity of the task. He handed each hot, clean dish to Cathy, who dried it with a sparklingly clean white towel, in the blue-and-white-tiled, Philippine-mahogany room.

For no real reason, a picture of Cathy the first time he had ever seen her came to Bill's mind—a small, square girl with chocolate cake and frosting all over her face and hands. It was during what he and Barbara ironically referred to as their courtship, a protracted and difficult period during which they had both been concerned with Bill's shedding his wife—and with the difficulty of seeing each other privately, what with Barbara's child and his wife. Barbara's first husband had moved to Dallas and had not seen Cathy since the divorce, but Barbara had felt that Bill and her daughter should not meet until Bill was actually free. So it was quite a while before Barbara could invite Bill for dinner. And on that occasion Cathy found the perfect, beautiful chocolate cake that Barbara had made and plunged her hands into its dark, moist depths, then smeared her face. Barbara had chosen to laugh rather than to scold, and Bill had liked her for that. Now the remembered sight of small, smeared Cathy moved him. He wanted to tell her about it, but he knew she would not understand; nor could she know that simply watching someone grow can make you care for them. So instead of any of that he said, "As a matter of fact I think James Fredericks is a jackass," and handed her a wet wineglass.

Carefully polishing, as she had been taught by her mother, Cathy asked, "Is he? I don't know."

"God, yes. All he can talk about is what he likes to call 'finances.' He can't say 'money.' Besides, you don't see his name on any anti-war petitions of doctors, do you? He probably owns stock in Dow Chemical."

Plunging his hands back into the sink, Bill realized that he had been wanting to say this for a long time. He had forgotten that Cathy was not supposed to know that he and Barbara had gone to Fredericks, and he wanted to reassure her, to tell her that if she didn't dig Fredericks it was certainly O.K. with him. But then he felt her mind float off to some clouded private distance of her own, and suddenly he couldn't stand it, and he turned furiously to confront her. "Listen," he said loudly, "you think you're confused, and that the world is difficult. Christ, what do you think it's like to be forty-one? Christ, talk about confused and difficult. Do you think I like getting outside myself and seeing a fatuous drunk whose scalp is beginning to show through? Christ! And believe me, being married is a hell of a lot more difficult than not being married, let me tell you. Your mother has to diet or she'd be fat, and she can't stand fat. And it's very hard to live without a lot of money and booze. You give it a little thought—just try."

Cathy's round eyes did not blink and she went on polishing the second wineglass. Then she glanced quickly at Bill and said, "O.K." Then she said, "I think I'll go to bed now," and Bill was left alone to clean the sink and wipe off the unvarnished wooden chopping table.

After he had finished that, he went into the small room off the living room that was known as his study; his books were there, and some portfolios of old drawings, and a collection of dirty pipes that he would have smoked only in that room. Now as he entered he found placed squarely in the middle of his desk a white sheet of paper, and on it were what he recognized as two joints.

He sat down in the comfortable green wool upholstered chair that Barbara had provided him, presumably for meditation, and he meditated, seeking a variety of explanations for Cathy's present, or gesture—whatever it was. However, nothing rational came to his mind. Or, rather, reasonable explanations approached but then as quickly dissolved, like clouds or shadows. Instead, salty and unmasculine tears stung at his eyes, and then he fell asleep in his chair, having just decided not to think at all.

Ripped Off

The gentle, leafy day made Deborah high; she came home from her morning job light in her head and heart. When she saw that the small drawer from her desk had been pulled out and taken over to the bed and left there, its contents spilled out over the tousled blue sheets, she first thought, Wow, Philip, what are you trying to tell me? Philip lived with her in the Russian Hill flat, and what was—or had been—in the drawer were notes from him, notes or bits of paper that for one reason or another he had put his name on or drawn some small picture on. A couple of the messages said "Gone for walk. Later." But on one, a torn-off match cover, he had written "I love you," and passed it to her across a table in a restaurant. There was even a canceled check made out to and endorsed by him, for a couple of months ago when Deborah had lent him some money.

Her second reaction was one of surprise; Philip was not nosy or jealous. Once she had known a boy, Juan, from Panama, who was both—violently so. She had had to burn her old letters and diaries so that he would not find them. In fact, he had finally left her because (he said) she was so friendly with other men. (She did not see herself as especially friendly to anyone.) It was not like Philip to search through her desk. She thought he must have been looking for a stamp or something. Still, why bring the drawer over to the bed? What was he trying to tell her?

Deborah was a tall, rather oddly shaped girl. Her breasts were large but her body was otherwise skimpy, and with her long thin legs she had somewhat the look of a bird that might topple over but never quite did. Big front teeth made her appear shy, which she was. Her wide dark-brown eyes could show a great deal of pain or love. She wore her brown hair long and straight, but for her Kelly Girl job—taken for two reasons: to give herself freedom of movement (she only took morning work), and to embarrass her mother, who expected her to have some kind of career—she dressed in short non-mini skirts and straight shirts. She tended to look for clothes that would hide her—hide her identity as well as her breasts. Her mother and some of the neighbors in that expensive San Francisco block—she and Philip lived in a building owned by Deborah's stepfather, who charged a ritualistic fifty a month for a high, wide studio room with an overwhelming view of the Bay and the ocean—described her as a hippie. Deborah felt that that was not quite right, although she could not have said what she was. She read a lot, and thought. Now she was mainly thinking about what to make for dinner for Philip, in case he came home for dinner.

As she picked up the bits of paper (nothing missing) and replaced the drawer and made the bed—bending awkwardly, tugging at the recalcitrant sheets—her discovery seemed less funny all the time. It was painful for Philip to know she was so sentimental. She blushed and pressed her fingers over her mouth. Nobody but a thirteen-year-old or a middle-aged woman (her mother, with all her dead father's Navy things, and pressed dead gardenias in a book of poems by Dorothy Parker) would keep stuff around like that. What would Philip think? Nothing between them was at all explicitly stated or defined. He had moved into the room shortly after they had met (at the Renaissance Fair, in Marin County—beautiful!) without much comment or any real plan, and he could presumably leave the same way. No one said anything about how long. Deborah sometimes thought he was there simply because of the coincidence in time between meeting her and the disbanding of his Mendocino commune and the start of a new term at the Art Institute. He was a little younger than she was—twenty-one to her twenty-three. His presence was kindly and peaceful, but he talked little, and it was not possible to tell what was in his mind. Sometimes he sang a line or two, like "It ain't me, babe, it ain't me you're looking for, babe." (Did he mean her?) Or, "Lay, lady, lay, lay across my big brass bed." (Had he met a new girl?)

As she straightened up from her own bed (the headboard of linen, not brass) she noticed what was incredible that she had not seen before: Philip had taken his zebra-skin rug. Loss hit her hard—so hard that she sat down on the bed and stared at the dusty space where the skins had been. He's used that silly drawer as an excuse to go, she thought. Of course. That was why he emptied it onto the bed. He was telling her that she was a terrible, possessive woman, hoarding souvenirs (like her mother), trying to hang on to him. The rug was the first thing he had brought over, by way of moving in, and despite their ambivalence about it (they disapproved of hunting, and too, the skins had a suggestion of decorator chic), it had picked up the look of the room, enhancing Deborah's wicker and white linen and black leather chairs—leavings from her mother's tasteful (the taste of five years back) country house.

Deborah was given to moments of total panic such as this, when the world seemed to lurch beneath her like the fun-house floor at Playland-at-the-Beach, when she gasped for air and found it hard to breathe. A psychiatrist had explained this tidily to her as a syndrome: she feared abandonment. Her father had gone off to war and been killed ("At three, you would have viewed this as a desertion—a deliberate one"), and it seemed (to the psychiatrist) that she tried to repeat that situation. She readily felt abandoned, and picked people who would abandon her, like Panamanian Juan. But no, she thought, she was at least able to make an effort to think things through in a reasonable way. She controlled her breathing (with Yoga breaths) and remembered that Philip had been talking about having the rug repaired. There was a rip in it that could get larger, or could trip one of them. It made sense— Philip finally took the rug off to be sewn. He had mentioned some people on Union Street who did things with hides and who had the right machines for skins.

Having decided so rationally on what had happened, Deborah felt better, but not very much better. Some cobweb of fear or anxiety clung to her mind, and she could not brush it off. She knew that she would not feel entirely well and reassured until she spoke to Philip. She concentrated on his phone call, which always came early in the afternoon, though by no stated arrangement. They would say whatever had happened in the day so far, and make some plan for the evening. Or Philip would say that he would see her later—meaning ten or eleven that night.

Naturally, since she was eager for Philip to call, several other people did instead, and each time her heart jumped as she answered, "Hello?"

Her mother said, "Darling, how are you? I was wondering if you and Philip are possibly free to come to dinner tomorrow? A couple of my professors from State are coming—you know, the ones who were out on strike—and I thought you might have fun with them."

Meaning: her mother thought the professors, who must have been quite young, would have a better time (and think better of her) if they met her hippie daughter with her long-haired, bearded boyfriend.

"Sure. I'll check with Philip," Deborah said, and then listened to her mother's continuing voice, which was grateful and full of love.

Once, when she was stoned, Deborah had said to Philip, "My mother's love comes at me like jelly. I have to be careful and stay back from it, you know? All that total approval I get poured over me. She doesn't even know who I am."

Philip's mother, in Cincinnati ("She pronounces it with a broad 'a'—can you imagine? Cincin*nah*ti." He, too, was a person displaced from the upper middle class), did not approve of him at all—his beard or his long hair, his Goodwill or Army-surplus clothes. Dropping out of Princeton to come to an art school in San Francisco. She had not been told about the commune in Mendocino; nor, presumably, about Deborah. "I don't mind her," he said. "She's sort of abrasive, bracing, like good sandpaper. She does her own thing, and it's very clear where we're both at."

Philip talked that hip way somewhat ironically, hiding behind it. "I think I'm what those idiot behavioral scientists call a post-hippie," he once said. "Sounds sort of like a wooden Indian, doesn't it?" But he had indeed put various things behind him, including drugs, except for an occasional cigarette. For him, Deborah had thrown out all her posters, and with him she had moved from Hesse and Tolkien to Mann and Dostoevski. "Let's face it, babe, they've got more to say. I mean, they've really got it all together."

After her mother's call, two friends called (about nothing), and finally there was the call from Philip.

She said, "Wow, Philip, what are you trying to tell me?" as she had planned to, but she felt no conviction.

"What?"

"The desk drawer on the bed."

"What drawer?"

" Did you take the zebra rug to be sewn?"

"No. Deb, are you trying to tell me that we've been ripped off, as they say?"

Crazily enough, this was a possibility she had not considered, but now she thought, Of course, it happens all the time.

'Debby," he was saying, "would you please look around and see what else is gone?"

As best she could, she did look around; she found her shoe box full of jewelry—the ugly inherited diamonds that she never wore—intact under her sweaters, and the stereo safely in its corner. The books, the records. His pictures. She came back to the phone and told him that.

"But aside from the stereo what else could they have taken?" she asked. "We don't have TV and appliances, stuff like that. Who wants our books?" She felt herself babbling, then said, "I'm really sorry about your rug."

"Oh, well. Maybe I wasn't supposed to have it."

"Shall I call the cops?"

"I guess. I'll be home for dinner, O.K.?"

Relief made Deborah efficient. Philip had not moved out, and he was coming home for dinner. She began to put together a rather elaborate lamb stew. (She always bought meat on the chance that he would come home, even though sometimes after several days of his absences she would have to throw it out.) She shaved fresh ginger into the lamb, and then she called the police.

The two officers who arrived perhaps twenty minutes later were something of a surprise. They were young— about her age. (Who of her generation would want to be a cop, she wondered.) One of them was blond and looked a little like a short-haired, clean-shaven Philip. They were quite sympathetic and soft-spoken; they gave sensible advice. "Use the double lock when you go out," the blond one said. "This one could be picked in a minute. And fix the bolt on the kitchen door."

"Do it soon," said the other. "They could be back for more."

"It's sort of funny they didn't take the stereo, too," Deborah said, conversationally.

"Hippies love those fur rugs," they told her, unaware that they were not talking to a nice girl from the right side of Russian Hill, and that for her they had just become the enemy.

"More likely junkies than hippies, don't you think?" she coldly said.

❦

For Deborah, the preparation and serving of food were acts of love. She liked to serve Philip; she brought in plates and placed them gently before him, like presents, although her offhand manner denied this.

"It's that Indian stuff," she said of the stew. Then, so that he would not be forced to comment on her cooking, she said, "It's funny, their moving that drawer from my desk."

"Probably thought you kept valuables there—bonds and bank notes and stuff." He was eating as though he were starved, which was how he always ate; he barely paused to look up and speak.

She felt herself inwardly crying, "I do! You are infinitely valuable to me. Anything connected with you

87

is valuable—please stay with me!" She managed not to say any of this; instead she blinked. He had been known to read her eyes.

"This stew is really nice," he told her. "And the wine—cool! Like wow!"

They both laughed a little, their eyes briefly meeting.

She asked, "How's school? How's the graphics class?"

"Pretty good."

Philip was thin, with knobby bones at his wrists, protuberant neck bones and tense tendons. He had dark-blue, thoughtful eyes. His fine hair flew about when he moved. He looked frail, as though a strong wind (or a new idea) could carry him off bodily. "I tend to get into head trips" is how he half ironically put it, not saying what kind of trips they were. He seemed to be mainly concerned with his work—drawing, etching, watercolors. Other things (people, weather, days) passed by his cool, untroubled but observant gaze—as someday, Deborah felt, she, too, might pass by.

At the moment, however, she was experiencing a total, warm contentment. There was Philip, eating and liking the stew she had made, and they had been robbed—ripped off—and nothing of value was gone.

"What was in the drawer?" he asked.

"Oh, nothing. Just some stuff I keep around."

Again their quick glances met, and they smiled; then both ducked away from prolonged contact. Deborah had to look aside because she had suddenly thought how marvelous it would be if they could have a child, a straw-blond baby that she would nurse (she had heard that breast-feeding made big breasts smaller) and Philip would always love. The intensity of this wish made her dizzy. For concealment, she asked, "You really won't miss those skins?"

"Really not. You know I always hated them as much

as I liked them. Good luck to whoever took them is how I feel."

❧⁓❧

After dinner Deborah cleared and cleaned the kitchen, while Philip read in the living room. Early on in their life together, he had helped or at least offered to, but gradually they both realized that cleaning up was something Deborah did not mind doing. She liked that simple interval of being alone, with nothing demanded of her that she could not accomplish. Her mother said of her that she was a throwback—"my quaint hippie daughter." Deborah supposed that there was something to that. She liked to polish the wine-glasses and to shine the chrome and porcelain on the stove and sink. She did all that tonight, and then went into the living room, where Philip was, and sat near him with a book of her own. With evening, the fog had begun to roll in. Outside, the distant foghorns announced a cold, moist black night. Wind shuddered against the windows, beyond which nothing was visible. The surrounding dark and cold made an island of their room—to Deborah, an enchanted island. She thought, We could live like this forever; this peace is better than any high. She thought, Do I want to get married, is that what I mean that I want? And then, No, I only mean to stay like this, with no change. But someday a baby.

They read for several hours. Absorbed in his book (*Doctor Faustus,* for the second time), Philip fought off sleep until he and then Deborah went into fits of yawns, and they gave up and went to bed.

While they were undressing, Deborah opened the drawer where she kept her scarves.

It was gone—her largest, most beautiful, pale striped silk scarf, all lavenders and mauves and pinks, the only present from her mother that she had ever liked. Wearing any dress at all, she could wrap herself in that scarf and be instantly elegant. Soon after she and Philip had met, she wore it to a party at the Institute, and he thought it was a wonderful scarf. The enormity of its absence had surely summoned her and made her for no reason open that drawer.

She felt hurt enough to cry, which, with a conscious effort, she did not do. Her second decision was not to tell Philip. This was less rational, and even as she slipped into bed beside him she was not sure why. Obviously, someday he would ask why she never wore it anymore. But at the moment she only knew that she felt diminished, as though without that scarf Philip would love her less, as though their best times together were over.

Philip turned on his side; having kissed her good night, he quickly fell asleep. She lay there in the dark, listening to the erratic mourning noise of the foghorns. She was thinking that even if she had a child he would grow up and go away. Finally, she couldn't stand it; all her thoughts were unbearable, and she turned and pressed her body against the length of Philip's slender warm back, holding him tightly with her arms, as though she could keep him there.

The Swastika on Our Door

Normally, Karen Washington took a warmly nostalgic interest in stories about and especially pictures of her husband's former girls. They had all been pretty, some beautiful. And they reminded her that her very successful and preoccupied lawyer husband had once been a lively bachelor, vigorously engaged in the pursuit of women. But the large glossy picture of Roger and his brother Richard, who was now dead, and a girl, that she found on the top shelf of her husband's shirt closet disturbed her considerably. Why had Roger put it there? She was not jealous; she did not suspect that he perpetuated an old liaison, but she felt left out. Why had he chosen not to tell her about this particular beautiful girl, in her high-collared coat?

To the left was fat Roger, grinning and blinking into the flashbulb, having raised his glass of wine to the nightclub camera: a man out on the town, celebrating, having a good time. "The jolly Roger": with his peculiar private irony Richard had sometimes called his brother that. On the right was skinny tortured Richard, who was staring at his brother with a gaze that was at the same time stern and full of an immoderate love. Between them, recessed into half shadow, was the long-necked beautiful dark girl, who was looking at Richard as though she thought he was either marvelous or crazy. Or perhaps she herself looked crazy. In the bright flat light her collar made an odd shadow on her cheek, and her eyes were a strange shape—very narrow and long, like fish.

Karen sighed heavily, and then sneezed from the dust. Although of German extraction she was a poor housekeeper, and did not like to be reminded of that fact, of which both the dust and the presence of that picture on an untouched shelf did remind her. Retreating from the closet, she put the picture on her husband's dressing table, meaning to ask him about it that night. She was a big dark handsome girl, descended from successful generations of Berlin bankers; her father, the last of the line, had come to San Francisco in the Twenties, well before Hitler, and had been prominent in the founding of a local bank. Karen had already, in ten years of marriage to Roger, produced five sons, five stalwart big Washingtons who did not remember their difficult doomed Southern uncle, Uncle Richard, cartons of whose books were still unpacked in the basement.

Karen remembered Richard very well, and she thought of him for a great deal of that day as she moved about the enormous unwieldy and expensive house on Pacific Street, bought when Richard died and they inherited his money. The house from its northern windows had mammoth views of the Bay, and the bridge, Sausalito, the hills of Marin County. That day, that March, there were threatening rain clouds, a shifting kaleidoscope of them, an infinite variety of grays.

Karen had felt and still did feel an uncomfortable mixture of emotions in regard to Richard, one of which was certainly the guilty impatience of the healthy with the sick. Richard had been born with a defective heart, ten months after Roger's healthy and very normal birth, and had suffered greatly during his lifetime. But beyond his irremediable physical pain he had seemed, somehow, to choose to be lonely and miserable. He lived in a strange hotel even after he got his money; he was given to isolated, hopeless love affairs, generally with crazy girls. ("Affairs with psychopaths are a marvelous substitute for intimacy," he had been heard to say.) He only bought books and records; his clothes were impossible.

Like many very secure and contented people, Karen tended to be somewhat unimaginative about the needs, emotional and otherwise, of those who were not content, of those who were in fact miserable. To her credit she knew this, and so she sighed as she moved incompetently about her house with the vacuum cleaner; she sighed for Richard and for her own failure to have understood or in any way to have helped him.

Karen's deficiencies as a housekeeper were more than made up for by her abilities as a cook, or so her greedy husband and most of their greedy friends thought. That afternoon, as heavy dark rains enshrouded the city and the Bay, Karen made a superior moussaka, which was one of Roger's favorites. It had also been a favorite of Richard's, and she was pleased to remember that she had at least done that for him.

Then, just as she had finished, from upstairs she heard the youngest child begin to whimper, waking up from his nap, and she went up to get him, to bathe and dress him before the older boys all tumbled home from school.

The maid would come at three and stay until after dinner, since Roger liked a formal evening meal.

Karen was dressing, and lost in a long skirt that she tried to pull down over big breasts, down over her increasing thighs, when Roger came in and asked her about the picture.

"What's that doing out here?" "Here" was "heah"; Roger had kept his Southern voice, though less strongly than Richard had.

Her head came out of the dress, and she bridled at the annoyance in his tone. "Why not? It was up on your top shirt shelf." At worst, in some atavistic Germanic way, Karen became coy. "Some old girl friend you haven't told me about?" she said.

Roger was holding the picture, blinking at it in the harsh light from Karen's makeup lamp, holding it closer and closer to the bulb as though he would burn it if the picture did not reveal all that he wanted to know. He was not thinking about Karen.

"She's beautiful," said Karen. She came to look over his shoulder, and pressed her cheek against his arm. She knew that he loved her.

"She was Richard's girl. Ellen. After that." He pointed unnecessarily at the picture. "We were celebrating his money, after he finally sold his land. That was the night he met her."

Karen was quiet, looking at the peculiar girl, and at Richard, whom no large sums of money had cheered, and at jolly Roger.

"What a creepy girl," Roger said. "Richard's worst. She finally had to be locked up. Probably still is."

"Oh." Karen shuddered.

Roger put the picture down with a heavy sigh. He was fatter now than when it was taken; his neck was deeply creased with fat, and his big cheeks drooped.

Then abruptly he turned around and embraced Karen with unaccustomed vigor. "What's for dinner?" he asked. "Did I smell what I think I did?"

❦

Because Richard had been sick so much and had been tutored, he and Roger ended by finishing high school in the same June of 1943, and that July they entered Harvard together, two Southern 4-F's in giddy wartime Cambridge, fat Roger, who also had a punctured eardrum, and thin sick Richard. They both reacted to that scene with an immediate and violent loneliness. Together they were completely isolated from all those uniforms, from the desperately gay urgency of that war, that bright New England climate.

Roger's fat and Richard's illnesses had also isolated them in childhood; they were unpopular boys who spent most of their afternoons at home, reading or devising private games. But to be isolated and unpopular in a small town where everyone knows you is also to be surrounded—if not with warmth at least with the knowledge of your history. There is always the old lady approaching on the sidewalk who says, "Aren't you Sophie Washington's boys? I declare, the fat one is the living spit of your grandfather." Or the mean little girl in the corner grocery store who chants softly, "Skinny and fat, skinny and fat, I never saw two brothers like that."

They had too an enormous retreat from the world: that huge house full of books everywhere. And the aging pale parents, Josiah and Sophie Washington, who had been and continued to be surprised at finding themselves parents, who retreated from parenthood to long conversations about the histories of other Southern families. "It was a perfect background for eccentrics of the future," Richard later told Ellen.

Both Roger and Richard had chosen history as their field of concentration at Harvard. During those summer afternoons, and into the gaudy fall, while R.O.T.C. units drilled in the Yard and pretty Radcliffe girls—in sloppy sweaters and skirts, white athletic socks and loafers—lounged on the steps of Widener Library, Richard and Roger studied furiously in their ground-floor rooms in Adams House, and at night they went to movies. Every night a movie, in suburbs as far-lying as the subway system would carry them, until one night when the only movie they had not seen twice was *I Wanted Wings*, in Arlington. So they stayed home and for a joke read chapters of *Lee's Lieutenants* aloud to each other, which was not one of the texts for History I but which was the only book in the room they had not already read. It had been an off-to-college present from their not very imaginative mother. In stage Southern accents they read to each other about Fredericksburg and Chickamauga, Appomattox and Antietam.

Roger had a photographic memory, of which Richard was wildly proud. His own memory was erratic; he easily memorized poetry but he had a lot of trouble with names and dates, with facts. As they walked across the Yard in the brilliant September air, Roger recited several pages from that book, still in that wildly exaggerated accent: ". . . and before the Northern armies could marshal their forces . . ." while Richard gamboled beside him, laughing like a monkey.

They were taking a course called Philosophic Problems of the Postwar World. With everyone else they stood around outside Emerson Hall, waiting for the hour to sound. Richard was overheard to say to Roger, in that crazy Southern voice, "As I see it, the chief postwar problem is what to do with the black people."

At the end of the summer Roger had four A's and Richard had two A's, a C and a D, the D being in Biology. They had no friends. Richard regarded their friendlessness as a sign of their superiority; no one else was as brilliant, as amusing, as his brother, and thus they were unappreciated. Roger didn't think much about that sort of thing then. He was solely concentrated on getting top grades.

Those Harvard years were, or perhaps became in memory, the happiest of Richard's life. Completely isolated from their classmates and from the war that for most people dominated the scene, he and Roger went about their scholarly pursuits; he had Roger's almost undivided attention, and it was a time when Roger laughed at all his jokes.

Aside from the Southern joke, which was their mainstay, they developed a kind of wild irony of their own, an irony that later would have been called sick, or black. Roger's obesity came into this. "You must have another hot dog, you won't last the afternoon," Richard would say as Roger wolfed down his seventh hot dog at lunch at the corner stand. And when Roger did order and eat another hot dog they both thought that wildly funny. Richard's heart was funny too. At the foot of the steps of Widener Roger would say, "Come on, I'll race you up to the top," and they would stand there, helplessly laughing.

That was how Richard remembered those years: big fat Roger, tilted to one side chuckling hugely, and himself, dark and wiry and bent double laughing, in the Cambridge sun. And he remembered that he could even be careless about his health in those years; he almost never hurt. They went for long walks in all the variously beautiful weathers of Cambridge. Years later, in seasonless California, Richard would sigh for some past Cambridge spring, or summer or fall. Roger remembered much less: for one thing he was in later life so extremely busy.

They were reacted to at Harvard for the most part with indifference; other people were also preoccupied, and also that is how, in general, Harvard is—it lets you alone. However, they did manage to be irritating: to the then current remark, " Don't you know there's a war on?" both Roger and Richard Washington had been heard to respond, "Sir, the War has been over for almost a hundred years." Also, those were very "liberal" years; racism, or what sounded like it, was very unpopular. No one made jokes about black people, no one but Roger and Richard.

Therefore, it is not too surprising that one night Roger and Richard came back from the movies (a revival of a *Broadway Melody* in Dorchester: Roger loved musicals) to find that someone had put a swastika in black chalk on the door to their room. Richard was absolutely enchanted; in a way it was the highest moment of his life. All his sense of the monstrosity of the outside world was justified, as well as his fondness for drama; he was persecuted and isolated with his brother. "Roger," he said very loudly and very Southernly, "do you reckon that's some kind of Indian sign they've gone and put on our door?"

Roger laughed too, or later Richard remembered Roger as laughing, but he recalled mainly his own delight in that climactic illuminated moment. They went into their room and shut the door, and after them someone yelled from down the stairwell, "Southern Fascists!" Richard went on chortling with pleasure, lying across the studio couch, while Roger walked thoughtfully about the room, that big bare room made personal only by their books and some dark curtains now drawn against the heady Cambridge spring night. Then Roger put a Lotte Lenya record on the player.

That was more or less that. The next day the janitor washed the chalk off, and Roger and Richard did not speculate as to who had put it there. Anyone could have.

But a week or so later Roger told Richard that he was tired of history; he was switching his field of concentration to economics. And then he would go to law school. "Fat makes you already eccentric," he said. "And eccentrics have to be rich."

"In that case I'll switch to Greek," Richard countered furiously, "and remain land poor."

And that shorthand conversation made perfect sense to both of them.

They both did what they said they would, except that soon after their graduation (Roger *summa cum laude* and Phi Beta) Richard had a heart attack that kept him in the hospital at home in Virginia, off and on for a couple of years, fending off his anxious mother and writing long funny letters to Roger, who seemed to be enjoying law school.

So it worked out that by the time Richard went back to Harvard for his master's in Greek literature, Roger had got out of law school and gone out to San Francisco, where he began to succeed as a management consultant to increasingly important firms. He was too busy even to come home for the funerals of his parents, who died within a month of each other during his first winter in San Francisco—Josiah and Sophie Washington, who had, they thought, divided their land equally between their two sons. Roger sold his immediately for thirty thousand, and thought he had done very well. He urged Richard to do the same, but Richard lazily or perversely held on to his, until the advent of a freeway forced him to sell, for a hundred thousand.

Richard did not enjoy his second time at Harvard, except in the sense that one does enjoy a season of mourning. He was terribly lonely, he missed Roger vividly, everywhere in Cambridge, and his heart hurt most of the time.

Thus it was not until the early Fifties that Richard got his teaching job in the boys' school in San Francisco, and came out to see his brother again. And then came into his money, and met Ellen.

In those days, even after getting his money, Richard lived in a downtown hotel—his eccentricity. He had a large room that the maid was not allowed to enter. ("In that case why live in a hotel?" practical Roger had asked.) The room was stacked everywhere with books, with records and papers. Richard took most of his meals in the hotel dining room; after he came home from a day of teaching he rarely went out. He was not well; much of the time he felt dizzy, and he ached, but again it was hard to gauge the degree to which his loneliness was chosen. If Roger, for example, had had a bad heart he would undoubtedly have had it continually in the midst of a crowd.

Indeed, in the years since his Harvard isolation Roger had become extremely gregarious. Professionally he was hyperactive; his entire intelligence and energy were occupied. And a vivid social life grew out of professional contacts. People whose adviser he was in a legal economic sense also asked him to dinner, and he became known as a very courtly, if somewhat ponderous bachelor, as well as an astute businessman. Roger was greedy for company; he reveled in all his invitations, his cocktails and dinners and his girls.

Girls who fell in love with Richard were always girls with whom Roger had not been successful; that was how Richard met girls. In one of their rare conversations about relationships with women, Roger remarked on Richard's perfect score with women; Richard had never been turned down.

"But with how many ladies have I—uh—attempted to prove my valor?" Richard asked, in the parody Southern manner that he sometimes tried to continue with Roger. "Four, or is it three? I sometimes lose track of these—uh—astronomicals."

Ellen made five.

One March afternoon, a few months after they had met, Richard lay across some tufts of new grass on the bank of a duck pond in Golden Gate Park, watching Ellen, who was out wading among the ducks. Like a child, she held her skirt bunched up in front of her, at the top of her long thin childish legs. Water still had spattered the shabby gray flannel; Ellen visibly didn't care. She splashed out toward some brown ducks who were peacefully squatted on the surface of the pond. They fled, scuttering across the water, submarining under, as Ellen screamed out, "See! They know I'm here!"

Her long fish eyes that day were almost blue with excitement. When she was unhappy or simply remote they were gray. After she finally went mad they were gray all the time.

At the farther edge of the pond were willows, now thickly green with spring; they grew out into the water in heavy clusters. And all about the pond were tall eucalyptus, scenting the air with lemon, shedding their bark in long strips, as the breeze fluttered their sad green scimitar leaves above Richard's heavy head.

Out of the water, out of her element, Ellen became a detached and languorous girl who sat on the grass not far from Richard, clutching her arms about her knees and watching him curiously, listening to that tormented and violent Southern talk.

"Interest! *Interest!*" was what Richard was saying. "My own brother, my *heir,* and he offers me interest on a loan. My God, I told him, 'You're my brother, take all the money, but for God's sake don't offer me interest.'"

Above the trees pale-gray clouds drifted ceremoniously across the sky. Half closing her eyes, Ellen turned them into doves, flocks and flocks of pale soft gray doves.

"God, if I'd only sold the bloody land when Roger sold his," said Richard for the tenth or perhaps the hundredth time that day. "And got only thirty thousand like him instead of this bloody hundred."

Richard's wildness and the intensity of his pain had oddly a calming effect on Ellen. Unlike most people, who were frightened or impatient or even—like

Roger—bored, Ellen experienced with Richard a re-
duction of the panic in which she normally lived.
Rather reasonably she asked him what she had often
been told but had forgotten: "Why didn't you sell it
then?"

"I preferred to be land poor." This was in the old
stage Southern voice. "Ah pruhfuhd." Then, "Christ, I
didn't want the money. I still don't. If I could only just
give it to him. Without dying, that is." And he laughed
wildly.

By this time pain had deeply lined Richard's face.
There were heavy lines across his forehead, lines down
the sides of his nose and beside his wide, intensely
compressed mouth. Many people, especially recent
friends of Roger's, considered Richard to be crazy, but
even they were aware that what sounded like madness
could have been an outcry against sheer physical
suffering.

"I may not even go to New York," Ellen said. "It
takes so much nerve."

Ellen was a mathematician—"of all things," as most
people said. Especially her Oakland-Baptist-John Birch
Society mother said that, and often. Ellen was talented
and had been offered a fellowship at Columbia.

"Stay here," Richard said. "Let me keep you. God,
won't anybody take my money?"

The melodramatic note in that last told Ellen that
Richard was going to talk about Roger again, and she
sighed. She liked it better when he was reading poetry
to her, or when he didn't talk at all and played records,
Telemann and Boccherini, Haydn and Schubert, in his
cluttered and most personal room.

But Richard said, "Roger wants to invest in some
resort land at Squaw Valley, with some of his rich new
German friends. Do you know the altitude at Squaw
Valley? Six thousand feet. I wouldn't last a minute
there. How to explain why his brother is never invited

for weekends or summer vacations. I am socially unacceptable to my brother—isn't that marvelous?"

Richard's eyes were beautiful; they were large and clear and gray, in that agonized face. Those eyes exposed all his pain and anger and despair, his eyes and his passionate deep Southern voice. He was really too much for anyone, and certainly for himself. And there were times, especially when he ranted endlessly and obsessively about Roger, when even Ellen wanted to be away from him, to be with some dull and ordinary person.

Ellen had met Roger, who always retained a few intellectual friends, at a Berkeley cocktail party, and she had had dinner with him a couple of times before the night they celebrated Richard's money at the silly expensive restaurant, where the picture was taken. Ellen had not liked Roger very much. He was exceptionally bright; she recognized and responded to that, but she was used to very bright people, and all the money-power-society talk that Roger tried to impress her with alarmed her. "You could marry extremely well if you wanted to," Roger told her. "With your skin and those eyes and those long legs. And no one should marry on less than thirty thousand a year. It can't be done." Then he had laughed. "But you'd probably rather marry a starving poet, wouldn't you? Come and meet my crazy brother, though, even if he has just come into money."

And so Richard and Ellen met, and in their fashions fell in love.

Now, feeling dizzy, Richard lay back on the bright-green grass and stared up through the lowering maze of silvered leaves to the gray procession of clouds. Sickness sometimes made him maudlin; now he closed his eyes and imagined that instead of the pond there was a river near his feet, the Virginia James of his childhood, or the Charles at Harvard, with Roger.

Not opening his eyes but grinning wildly to himself, he asked Ellen, "Did I ever tell you about the night they put the swastika on our door?"

Of course Richard lent Roger the money, with no interest, and their dwindling relationship continued.

Sometimes even in the midst of his burgeoning social life Roger was lonely; he hated to be alone. Sometimes late at night he would telephone to Richard, who always stayed up late reading and playing records. These conversations, though never long, were how they kept in touch.

At some point, a couple of years after Richard had met Ellen, Roger began to talk about a girl named Karen Erdman, and Richard knew that she was the one he would marry. But Roger took a long time deciding—Karen was a patient girl. Richard did not meet Karen until the engagement party, but he was so intuitively attuned to his brother that he could see her and feel the quality of her presence: that big generous and intelligent girl who adored his brother. After all, Richard also loved Roger.

"The question seems to me," advised Richard, "as to whether you want to marry at all. If you do, obviously Karen is the girl you should marry."

"I have a very good time as a bachelor," Roger mused. "But it takes too much of my time. You break off with one girl and then you have to go looking for another, and at first you have to spend all that time talking to them."

"God, what a romantic view. In that case perhaps you should marry."

"But she wants children. I find it almost impossible to imagine children."

"Sir, what kind of a man would deplore the possibility of progeny?" Richard asked, in their old voice.

"I can't decide what to do," said Roger. Then, as an afterthought: "How is Ellen?"

"Marvelous. She has managed to turn down four fellowships in one year."

"She's crazy."

"You're quite right there."

"Well. Good night."

"Good night."

A heavy engraved invitation invited Richard to the Erdman's engagement party for their daughter. "Oddly enough," Richard said to Ellen. "Since they're being married at Tahoe I'm surprised they didn't do the whole thing up there. Or simply not mention it till later. God knows I don't read the society pages."

Richard was not asked to bring Ellen.

The Erdman house, in Seacliff, was manorial. Broad halls led into broader, longer rooms; immense windows showed an enormous view of the Bay. And the décor was appropriately sumptuous: satins and velvets and silks, walnut and mahogany and gilt. Aubusson and Louis XV. For that family those were the proper surroundings. They were big dark rich people who dressed and ate and entertained extremely well.

In those crowded, scented, overheated rooms Richard's pale lined face was wet. He went out so infrequently; the profusion and brilliance of expensive clothes, in all possible fabrics, of jewels—all made him dizzily stare. The acres of tables of incredibly elaborate food made him further perspire. He stood about in corners, trying to cope with his dizziness and wildly wondering what he could find to say to anyone there. Lunatic phrases of gallantry came to him. Could he say to the beautiful blonde across the room, "I just love the way you do your hair, it goes so well with your shoes"? Or, to the tall distinguished European, who was actually wearing his decorations, "I understand you're in money, sir. I'm in Greek myself. Up to my ass in Greek." No, he could not say anything. He had nothing to say.

Roger's new circle included quite a few Europeans, refugees like his father-in-law to be, and Mr. Erdman's friends, and transients: visiting representatives of banks, commercial attachés and consuls. The rest were mainly San Francisco's very solid merchant upper class: German Jewish families who had had a great deal of money for a long time. They were very knowledgeable about music and they bought good paintings on frequent trips to Europe. Among those people Roger looked completely at home; even his heavy Southern courtliness took on a European flavor.

Mrs. Erdman was still a remarkably pretty woman, with smooth dark hair in wings and round loving eyes as she regarded both her husband and her daughter. Richard found this especially remarkable; he had never known a girl with a nice mother and he imagined that such girls were a breed apart. Ellen's mother had jumped under a train when Ellen was thirteen and miraculously survived with an amputated foot.

Mrs. Erdman was a very nice woman and she wanted to be nice to Richard, once it was clear to her who he was. The two boys were so unlike that it was hard to believe. "I'm so sorry that you won't be able to come up to the lake for the wedding," she said sympathetically.

"But who'd want a corpse at a wedding?" Richard cackled. "Where on earth would you hide it?" Then, seeing her stricken face and knowing how rude he had been, and how well she had meant, he tried again: "I just love the way you do your hair—" But that was no good either, and he stopped, midsentence.

Mrs. Erdman smiled in a vague and puzzled way. It was sad, and obvious that poor Richard was insane. And how difficult for poor Roger that must be.

Roger was beaming. His creased fat face literally shone with pleasure, which, for the sake of dignity, he struggled to contain. Having decided to marry, he found the idea of marriage very moving, and he was impressed by the rightness of his choice. People fall in love in very divergent ways; in Roger's way he was now in love with Karen, and he would love her more in years to come. He was even excited by the idea of children, big handsome Californian children, who were not eccentric. He stood near the middle of the enormous entrance hall, with Karen near his side, and beamed. He was prepared for nothing but good.

Then suddenly, from the midst of all that rich good will, from that air that was heavy with favorable omens, he heard the wild loud voice of his brother, close at hand. "Say, Roger, remember the night they put the swastika on our door?"

There was a lull in the surrounding conversations as that terrible word reverberated in the room. Then an expectant hum began to fill the vacuum. Feeling himself everywhere stared at, and hearing one nervous giggle, Roger attempted a jolly laugh. "You're crazy," he said. "You've been reading too many books. Karen, darling, isn't it time we went into the other room?"

It is perhaps to the credit of everyone's tact that Richard was then able to leave unobtrusively, as the front door opened to admit new guests.

And a month later, two months before the June wedding at Lake Tahoe, Richard had a severe heart attack and died at Mount Zion Hospital, with Ellen and Roger at his bedside.

They had been watching there at close intervals for almost the entire past week, and they were both miserably exhausted. Even their customary wariness in regard to each other had died, along with Richard.

"Come on, let me buy you some coffee," said Roger, fat and paternal. "You look bad."

"So do you," she said. "Exhausted. Thanks, I'd like some coffee."

He took her to a quiet bar in North Beach, near

where she was then living, and they sat in a big recessed booth, in the dim late-afternoon light, and ordered espresso. "Or would you like a cappuccino?" Roger asked. "Something sweet?"

"No. Thanks. Espresso is fine."

The waiter went away.

"Well," said Roger.

"Well," echoed Ellen. "Of course it's not as though we hadn't known all along. What was going to happen."

The flat reasonableness of her tone surprised Roger. Ellen was never reasonable. So he looked at her with a little suspicion, but there was nothing visible on her white face but fatigue and sadness. The strain of her effort at reasonableness, at control, was not visible.

Roger said, "Yes. But I wonder if we really believed it. I mean Richard talked so much about dying that it was hard to believe he would."

The coffee came.

Stirring in sugar, regarding her cup, Ellen said, "People who talk about jumping under trains still sometimes do it. But I know what you mean. We somehow didn't behave as though he would die. Isn't that it?" She lifted her very gray eyes to his blinking pale blue.

He took the sugar, poured and stirred. "Yes, but I wonder what different we would have done."

In her same flat sensible tone Ellen said, "I sometimes wouldn't see him when he wanted to. I would be tired or just not up to it, or sometimes seeing someone else. Even if the other person was a boring nothing." She looked curiously at Roger.

But he had only heard the literal surface of what she had said, to which he responded with a little flicker of excitement. "Exactly!" he said. "He was hurt and complained when I went to boring dinners or saw business friends instead of him, but I had to do that. Sometimes for my own protection."

"Yes," said Ellen, still very calm but again with an oblique, upward look at Roger, which he missed.

"People grow up and they change." Roger sighed. "I could hardly remember all that time at Harvard and he always wanted to talk about it."

"Of course not," she said, staring at him and holding her hands tightly together in her lap, as though they contained her mind.

Roger was aware that he was acting out of character; normally he loathed these intimate, self-revelatory conversations. But he was extremely tired and, as he afterward told himself, he was understandably upset; it is not every day that one's only brother dies. Also, as he was vaguely aware, some quality in Ellen, some quality of her listening, drove him on. Her flat silence made a vacuum that he was compelled to fill.

"And remember that time a couple of years ago when I wanted to borrow the money?" Roger said. "He was so upset that I offered him interest. Of course I'd offer him interest. Otherwise it wouldn't have been fair."

"Of course not," said Ellen, looking deeply into his eyes. "Everyone has to pay interest," she reasonably said.

"It was the least I could do," Roger said. "To be fair to him. And I couldn't spend the rest of my life thinking and talking about how things were almost twenty years ago."

"Of course not," Ellen said again, and soon after that he took her home and they parted—friends.

But in the middle of that night Roger's phone rang, beside his wide bachelor bed, and it was Ellen.

"Pig pig pig pig pig pig pig pig pig!" she screamed. "Horrible fat ugly murdering pig, you killed him with your never time to see him and your wall of fat German business friends always around you and your everything for a purpose and your filthy pig-minded greed and your all-American pig success and your so socially acceptable ambitions. Richard was all Greek to you and you never tried to learn him, how lovely he was and suffering and you found him not socially acceptable to your new society and your new pig friends and I would even rather be thin and miserable and ugly me than fat you with your blubber neck and your compound interest and you couldn't believe his heart and now you can get filthy blubber fatter on his money—"

She seemed to have run down, and into the pause Roger asked, "Ellen, do you need money? I'd be more than happy—"

She screamed, but it was less a scream than a sound of total despair, from an absolute aloneness.

Then she hung up, and a few weeks later Roger heard that she had had a complete breakdown and was hospitalized, perhaps for good.

❧

After the excellent dinner of moussaka, salad and strawberries in cream, Karen and Roger settled in the living room with strong coffee and snifters of brandy. It was an attractive, comfortable, if somewhat disheveled room, very much a family room. Karen's tastes were simpler than those of her parents. Her furnishings were contemporary; the fabrics were sturdy wools or linen; the broad sofa was done in dark-brown leather.

Roger leaned back; he blinked and then sighed, looking up to the ceiling. Karen could tell that he was going to say something about Richard.

"I sometimes wish," said Roger, "that I'd taken the time somewhere along the line to have learned a little Greek. It seemed to give Richard so much pleasure."

"But, darling, when would you ever have had the time?"

"That's just it, I never had the time." Roger's tone when talking about or in any way alluding to his brother was one of a softly sentimental regret; Karen gathered that he regretted both his brother's death and their lack of rapport in those final years.

Roger also sounded sentimentally regretful when he referred to anything cultural—those soft pleasures which he valued but for which he had never had time.

"I wonder what's ever happened to that girl. Ellen," said Karen.

"I'm not sure I'd even want to know," said Roger. "Did I ever tell you that she called me the night he died?"

"Really? No."

"Yes, she was quite hysterical. I think she was angry because she knew I was Richard's heir." By now Roger had come to believe that this was indeed the case. He was convinced that other people's motives were basically identical to his own. "Yes," he said. "She probably thought I should give her some of his money."

In the large safe room, beneath other large rooms where her sons were all sleeping, Karen shuddered, and together she and Roger sighed, for Richard's pain and death and for poor lost Ellen's madness.

"Here," said Karen, "have more coffee. Poor darling, you look as though you need it."

"You're right. I do." And Roger reached out to stroke his big wife's smooth dark cheek.

A Jealous Husband

On being told that his wife was having an affair with a black orderly in the hospital where she worked, Stuart Macmillan experienced great rage and a piercing anguish; and also, to almost the same degree, he felt vastly surprised. It was not something that he would ever have expected of Martha.

To begin with, she was plump. Although her face was smooth and pretty, her body ballooned out above short legs. "The thalidomide kid" was how she sometimes referred to herself. She had a quick mean mind that always appealed to Stuart. But one of his reactions was that she had been singled out for love.

Aside from the fast that he liked her face and her head, Stuart had probably singled her out at least partly because he was fairly funny-looking too. He was tall and scrawny, with small bright eyes and a long scraggly black beard. He moved along lopingly, like a bird that might take off into flight. As a couple they appealed to most people's sense of humor, including their own, but somehow Stuart did not think the black orderly had chosen Martha for laughs.

Stuart and Martha were from a medium-sized city in Virginia, and there they had gone to high school together, and halfway through college, until simultaneously they decided to drop out and head West, and, more or less incidentally, to marry. Apart from their somewhat freakish looks, the circumstance that made them friends was their I.Q.s, known city-wide as staggeringly high. Thus they were alone together at the top of the class, sharing prizes and similarly poor at sports or dancing. They were known locally as hippies, in a town that the hippie movement had totally bypassed.

The town also viewed Stuart's attachment to Martha as a sign of great virtue—in him. This very Southern and sexually chauvinistic view stemmed from a theory that such a fat girl was lucky to have a beau at all; it ignored Stuart's equal (in conventional terms) unattractiveness. Martha should be grateful, and the fact that she was not, that she was mean to Stuart, made him look even better to the town. "That boy must be a saint to put up with that mean old fat little girl" was the general view.

"Go peddle your masochism" was what Martha sometimes said to Stuart, and he had to admit that there was something to her theory.

But he argued: "Your self-hatred is really the problem. You think anyone who digs you is crazy, of all the banal female hang-ups."

Most of their conversation, and their fights, took place in an outlandish bar just out of town called the Porthole. They chose it for its sheer dreadfulness, from the dingy brass rail around the roof outside to the jaunty saltshaker that was in the shape of a sailor boy. They also liked it because no one they knew from school would ever have dreamed of going there. They sat drinking beer, which made Stuart moody and introspective, and which only added to Martha's fat.

She had long straight brown hair that streaked blond in the summer, big dark-blue eyes and smooth tan skin. In his simpler moments Stuart thought he dug her because she was so pretty—reason enough for a healthy Virginia boy. But his simple moments were few. Having gone from Alan Watts to Ouspensky and back and forth to Camus and Kierkegaard, he was very much hung up on levels of awareness, on consciousness. Whey was he obsessed with a mean fat girl who didn't especially like him? Even if her I.Q. was almost as high as his own, why did his stomach seem to contort at a sudden chance sight of her?

On certain levels they got along very well. They both regarded the city where they lived, and actually most of the South, with a sort of total outrage. "It's *absurd,* it is absolutely absurd," said Stuart, who had also been reading Sartre, and they laughed, aghast, at politicians who spoke out on miscegenation and small-town sheriffs who shot black people. They did not, however, associate themselves with any of the radical groups, such as they were, in the area; neither of them could have functioned in a group.

Then gradually over the summer, as they discussed themselves and the world, Stuart began to feel that Martha liked him better, particularly when they were not talking about how they felt about each other, a subject that always made her edgy. Sometimes in the back seat of Stuart's car they made love, which was not a tremendous success for either of them—but better than fighting, Stuart thought.

By the end of the summer they had exhausted their surroundings as a focus for contempt, and so Stuart said the logical next thing: "Why do we stick around here, then? Why don't we head for San Francisco?" And, almost as an afterthought, "The trip would be easier if we got married."

But marriage, as it will, changed their relationship considerably, perhaps even more than the move to San Francisco did. Now that they were legally joined, and living under a single roof, their lives seemed to diverge.

Their apartment was the top floor of an old house out on Valencia Street. Some homing instinct must have led them there, for it had very much the look of a Southern country house, with its bay windows and narrow side porch; there were even columns overgrown with wisteria. They chose it instantly, and gave the last of their savings, on a two-year lease, to the Mexican woman whose house it was. Their apartment was cut up into useless small rooms, but the back windows overlooked a small apple and cherry orchard, and from the front they could sometimes see as far as the Bay.

Their ways began to separate when Martha, almost immediately, found an excellent job as a medical secretary in one of the larger private hospitals. Whereupon Stuart slackened the pace of his search, which hadn't been vigorous to begin with. Martha, diligent and compulsive, had to leave for work at 8:45, since the hospital was in a distant neighborhood. Stuart slept late, and perused the want ads over his breakfast and coffee. There was seldom anything that promised much; also, being exceptionally shy, Stuart could hardly bear the thought of presenting himself to anyone, and, finally, the reading of ads became his sole form of job-hunting.

Each day, after he had showered and got into clean jeans and a shirt, he went out into the city, his heart swelling as it once had at the prospect of seeing Martha. In fact, marrying Martha had largely released him from his obsession with her; he now loved her without anxiety. He was free to fall in love again, and he fell in love with the city. He became a passionate walker, a watcher of everything, everyone, every place. He walked through the Mission District to Market Street, idling among the sailors and shoppers, the freaks and drunks; he went from Union Square through Chinatown to North Beach, then across Russian Hill and along Union Street, up to Pacific Heights and out to Golden Gate Park, observing in detail each person and animal and tree. He was literally intoxicated by the city.

He was still reading a lot, and thinking, and he often felt that he was on the verge of giant realizations. It seemed the happiest period of his life.

Although older people may have taken him for a hippie, he was not regarded as one by the hippies themselves, who were able to recognize their own. They knew that Stuart was something else.

One of the things that excited him about the city was the variety of available foods, and it became his habit to bring home treats for dinner. He brought fresh ravioli, egg rolls and tortillas, bread from North Beach and cracked crab from Fisherman's Wharf. While Martha, exhausted from work and standing up on buses, took off her shoes and lay back on the mohair sofa with a book, Stuart made their dinner.

During the meal, conversation was mainly about what they were eating: where it came from, how much it had cost and how it compared to their recent gastronomic adventures.

Martha usually went to bed right after dinner, while Stuart stayed up to read. Sometimes, for love, he woke her when he came to bed, and she was usually nice about it, but it was nothing terrific, not what he would have imagined love should be.

Later, after his terrible discovery, Stuart focused on that first year of their marriage, recognizing that he really had not paid much attention to her. He lacerated himself for that, and also for letting her work at a demanding job while he lay around in parks all day. They both could have got part-time jobs; an arrangement like that would have been more just, he later thought.

Also, he searched the past for clues that might have told him what Martha had been doing, but he found very few. Martha had read a lot of books about black people; she read Claude Brown and Cleaver and Malcolm X, but a lot of people read those books that year. At times she made sounds of discontent; once she had said, "I really wonder why we came out here!" But Martha had always sounded discontent. And her fatigue was readily explained by work and public transportation. Stuart was never able to find anything that might have prepared him for the phone call which came one Friday morning.

A black girl's voice asked: "This Stuart Macmillan? Your wife works over to the hospital?"

"Yes." Anticipating everything but what he actually heard, still Stuart held his breath.

The girl's voice rose, became shrill: "You tell your wife stop messing around with my old man—you tell her leave Jackson Walker alone!"

"What? What're you talking about?"

"You heard me!" By then the girl was screaming. "He got stoned and told me, stoned and bragging on his white chick—you tell her stop!" And she hung up in Stuart's ear.

Stuart, who had been standing up, sat down. He sat upright, his back hard against the chair, as though impaled there by what he had heard. Then slowly he got up to take his shower and to dress, as usual.

It was an exceptionally beautiful April day, warm and clear. Stuart took a book to Golden Gate park and lay there on a grassy, sheltered knoll. He watched a group of black boys with natural hair, and he wondered

117

why his chest tightened at the sight of them, until he remembered the phone call.

He thought he was reading, then noticed that his book was upside down. He went home without buying any treats for supper.

When Martha came in, he stopped her near the door. Gripping her shoulders, he shouted at her, "What do you mean, screwing that black guy? What do you mean?"

"What are you talking about?" But she began to tremble within his grasp, and her blue eyes widened.

"Who's Jackson Walker, then? Christ, did he have to tell his wife? Did I have to hear about it? Christ, how dare you!"

In a tiny voice she said, "I thought you didn't like me anymore."

"Christ, you dumb trite bitch!" He hit her then, as hard as he could, across the face—twice, so that the palm of his hand stung.

Her face was instantly imprinted with scarlet. He saw his harsh mark on her delicate skin, and he began to cry, as she did, and he took her in his arms. Somehow, then, they moved toward the bedroom, the bed. Martha was still crying. Stuart had stopped. He undressed her, then himself, and then he made love to her, with a fury, with an abandon so wild he could never have imagined himself capable of it.

Later that night he went out and got hamburgers, which they ate in bed, and then they made love again.

❧

The next day, as he perused the paper, Stuart saw an ad that appealed to him. "Carpenter's assistant, Potrero Hill, $2.50 hr." And a phone number to call. The money was of course absurd, but he liked the idea of carpentry and he liked Potrero Hill, with its wide bare streets and its views of the industrial district and the Bay. He called and was given an address, to which he went and found a very small Italian carpenter, Mario, who hired him on the spot, "So tall a boy! Such a help to Mario!" and they spent a pleasant afternoon together, putting up shelves in a house that some professors were remodeling.

"What he really wants, of course, is a son," Stuart said to Martha, over dinner.

"Well, don't knock it." This seemed very funny to them, in their nervous state; they both laughed.

❦

With his first day's wages—Mario paid daily, in cash, with no deductions—Stuart took Martha out to dinner. Being out together in a dim North Beach restaurant combined with the melodrama of the night before to make them both nervous; they were slightly unreal to each other. They laughed a lot, like people on a "date," and they ate very little, like people recently in love.

They did not explicitly discuss what had happened between Martha and the orderly. But as Stuart looked at her across the table, and later when he held her in his arms, he experienced a pain so intense that it was almost sweet, at the thought of Martha with another man, another man who had seen and touched her naked, who had heard her laugh and cry out. The thought stabbed into his chest, then gripped his stomach like a hard cold hand.

In a way he wanted to ask Martha and to have her tell him all the details of the affair, as though sharing it would exorcise his pain. But he knew that he could not have borne to hear about it. And so he tortured himself with trying to imagine how it had been. He wondered where they went to do it—then remembered that hospitals are full of rooms with beds.

119

Sometimes what made him angriest was the relationship that Martha had created between him and that black man, that Jackson Walker. What contempt Walker must feel for him, Stuart thought: for a man whose wife would cheat on him after less than two years of marriage. What had she said about him? Once or twice he awoke in the night enraged by such thoughts, and decided that he would have to fight Jackson Walker, whom he imagined to be stronger, heavier, much better built than himself.

But, aside from the hell that he created frequently inside his head, Stuart's life with Martha went into a golden, halcyon phase.

For one thing, the seventy or eighty dollars a week that he brought home meant money to spare. Unused to having extra cash, he put it in a bank, and then one day, on impulse, he bought a car, a completely characterless 1955 Chevrolet that turned out to have a very good engine. He and Martha began to explore the countryside. Every weekend, all during that sunny spring, they drove somewhere, taking picnics of cheese and bread, fruit and wine.

Once on a Sunday late in June, they headed for the wine country. Put off by the crowds of tourists lined up to go through the big wineries, they struck out on a narrow white dirt road that ran through some green vineyards, and suddenly, at a bend in the road, they came upon a big square stone building, covered with rippling green leaves, probably an abandoned winery. They stopped the car and got out, and then, as they approached the building, a white owl flew out from a high small window. It disappeared in an instant, so quickly that they were not quite sure they had actually seen it; nevertheless it was an image that stayed in their minds, along with that of the lovely romantic vine-covered stone, and the enormous bay tree, beneath which they spread their blanket and ate and drank their picnic. Years later one of them would ask the other, "Do you remember the white owl we saw?" Meaning: do you remember that afternoon under the bay tree?

Because he was so close to her, Stuart seldom really looked at Martha, but partly because of the newness of this place, he did so now, and he saw that the lines of her face had slightly changed: more bones showed, and bones showed even along her thigh as she sat with her legs bent to one side, her denim skirt taut.

"Hey," he said, "you've got thin."

"Well, not exactly thin," she said. "Don't lose your head over a couple of pounds." But she smiled, very pleased with herself and with him, and she poured out more wine.

They were sitting near the stone building on a large plateau, above the vineyard, commanding a view of the green flowing vines that stretched for miles beneath the hot June sky, back to the highway. The warm air smelled winey, and was sweetened with bay leaves and stray flowers. Stuart had brought two joints, and as they smoked the scene became more fluid and brighter green, the wine scent stronger.

At some point a large yellow dog ambled up to them, where they lay on their spread-out blanket. He had a black spot that surrounded one eye—a cartoon of a dog.

"I'll bet anything I know what your name is," Martha told the dog, who sniffed the air suspiciously, gave them a long hard look, then suddenly turned and dashed off down the road.

This visitation, combined with the effect of the dope, made Martha and Stuart laugh like maniacs; they lay back on the blanket and laughed until their stomachs hurt and tears ran down their cheeks. It was a memorably long afternoon, and finally they fell asleep, curled up together like kittens.

Later, waking abruptly, his arms still holding his soft

and pretty wife, Stuart was struck with a dark and terrible thought: for all he knew, Martha was still seeing (meaning screwing) Jackson Walker. Since their reconciliation—renewal would be the more accurate word—he had simply assumed her affair was over. Nevertheless, how could he be sure? What had she said? He was *not* sure, and that uncertainty caused a pain in his chest like that of angina, sharp, and hard to bear.

But as Martha woke and turned, smiled and kissed his face, the pain retreated, only to return from time to time (somewhat diminished) as all his worst thoughts did.

Their good life continued through the summer. Stuart went on working with Mario, enjoying his increasing skill; the fact that he was earning money with his hands appealed to him. And he was happy with Martha, who seemed to grow prettier and somewhat thinner—at least less fat—all the time. These days it was Martha who made dinner, since he got home later and was often more exhausted than she. She made wonderful stews and heavy soups, and she had a special skill with salads: she put everything into them and all the crisp flavors were glorious together.

But Stuart was still tortured by his thoughts; they obsessed him as Martha herself had, in their old pre-marriage days. He had frequent horrible fantasies about her with the black man, with Jackson Walker. He did not consider the fact of Walker's blackness to be important; he was sure he would have felt just as terrible no matter who it had been. And he had read enough Freud to question his obsession; he knew about the homosexual implications of jealousy. Did he, a nice white Southern boy, secretly yearn for sexual union with a black man? He searched out his heart and his id, but honestly could not see how this theory applied to him.

122

Sometimes he imagined asking Martha very calmly some questions about the affair—for instance, how and when it had ended. But as he phrased the questions to himself, his calm departed and his chest vibrated with anxiety.

The only time they had anything resembling a conversation about her defection was after a party that Mario gave. It was a huge mixed bag of a party: Mario collected people. It was presided over by Esther, Mario's wife, a placid blond giant of a woman. (Meeting her, Stuart had felt much closer to Mario: he understood about a mania for one's physical antethesis.) And Mario's guests seemed to have been invited for variety's sake: there were two hippie girls with long blond hair, a middle-aged Spanish painter with his young Greek wife, three young black men with naturals, an octogenarian woman sculptor, a homosexual real-estate dealer, two timid boys who worked for the Welfare Department and an elegant black woman social worker. And Martha and Stuart.

To all these people Esther ladled out a watery stew as though it were marvelous, and she smiled blandly to conceal her dislike of them all. She loved Mario, but hated parties and most people. She turned up the volume of the stereo, which blared rock music into the room, and she kept refilling the glasses with cheap red wine. Since there had not been quite enough to eat, everyone got smashed, especially the people who were also smoking dope in the basement.

Having temporarily lost sight of Martha, Stuart talked to the black woman social worker. He asked her about the mayor's plans for Hunter's Point.

"What plans?"

Stuart wandered away, and eventually downstairs. There it was dark and sweet with smoke; the Beatles blasted out "Good Day, Sunshine!" At first he couldn't find Martha, but then he did see her, dancing with a tall black man, shyly thrusting her pelvis in and out, her body writhing in response to the man's more violent motion. All their contortions were perfectly synchronized; they might have been dancing together for years. Stuart and Martha never danced well together, and watching those two was more than Stuart could stand. He pushed his way through the group on the stairs and walked out of the house.

He was confused about where he had parked the car, and before he could find it, Martha found him. They got into the car from opposite sides and sat there, not facing each other. Stuart did not start the motor.

They were high up on Potrero Hill, overlooking the darkened warehouse area. In silence they watched the bright stream of traffic along the Embarcadero, until Stuart said, "How can I trust you—ever again? How do I know you won't find someone again?" He spoke hesitantly; saying those words was very painful to him.

She was as slow to answer. "Well," she said, and he could see the gleam from the streetlight reflected in her serious eyes, "I suppose you can't. But you could find someone too, you know. Who can promise anyone?"

"God, thanks a lot for being so honest!"

"Don't you want me to be?"

"Of course not!" screamed Stuart, who was, in his way, considerably more honest than she.

They drove home in silence.

❧

During the period of his obsession with Martha's infidelity, Stuart often woke at three or four in the morning. Unable to sleep, he brooded about Martha and Jackson Walker, trying to imagine them together. So intense was his concentration, he sometimes felt that he was on the verge of actually seeing them. But one morning in February, at 3 A.M.—it was terribly dark, and a cold wet wind misted the windowpanes—he tried, as he had often tried, to discover why he spent so much time thinking about such a painful subject.

And then a frightening thought occurred to him: perhaps he was in love with Martha's love affair?

It was as though an oracle had made the pronouncement. It had the ominous echo of total truth. The next day he felt tired and raw and depressed. He drank too much wine with Mario at lunch, and in the middle of dinner that night he fell asleep in his chair.

During the next few weeks, as the weather turned springlike and daphne bloomed in the garden below their window, Stuart began to regard himself with intense suspicion: now that he had found himself out, would the marriage fall apart? Had he, in truth, lost interest in Martha, since presumably she was no longer having the affair that had provided him with such orgies of jealous pleasure?

By April he had decided that his fears had been groundless. They still lived together fairly happily; they had a good time talking and sleeping together. One day he realized that he had not thought about Jackson Walker for weeks, and it struck him, too, that he missed his old preoccupation.

That night at dinner, as coolly as he could, he said, "I suppose your former black friend had a natural out to there?" And he gestured out from his own small head.

At first she looked surprised, and then she narrowed her eyes as though with an effort either at recollection or at fathoming her husband. "No," she finally said, "it was pretty short."

That information was enough to rekindle Stuart's fantasies; for the next few weeks he was frequently shot through again with the sweet piercing pain that accompanied his image of Martha touching and caressing another man's hair.

But gradually this phase too passed. The whole

episode began to seem quite remote, and Stuart became desperate without it. And so, on another night at dinner, he braced himself, and asked, "I suppose all that stuff about black men being so great in the sack is a lot of bull?"

Again, considering, she narrowed her eyes, and it came to Stuart that she looked like the mean old Martha who had sat across from him in the Porthole, at home, putting down his love. Then, "No," she said, quite deliberately, "as a matter of fact he was wild."

Stuart got up and hit her across the mouth.

Flights

"Oh, yes, Valerie will like it *very much,*" said the energetic young man with blue-black hair and a sharply cleft chin, in an accent that was vaguely "English." He and Jacob Eisenman were standing in the large shabby room that overlooked the crashing Pacific, on Kauai, one of Hawaii's outermost and least populated islands.

Jacob later thought that the implications of his tone were a sort of introduction to Valerie, although at the time he had not entirely understood what was being implied. Jacob, the gaunt sardonic literary German who, incongruously, was the owner of this resort. Then he simply wondered why, why *very much?* The young man's clothes were pale, Italian, expensive; it was unlikely that he (or Valerie) would be drawn by the price, which was what drew most of the other guests: older people, rather flabby and initially pale, from places like North Dakota and Idaho and, curiously, Alaska—and a few young couples, wan tired families with children. These people stayed but were not enthusiastic; they would have preferred a more *modern* place. (Jacob was subject to radar intuitions.) And so this young man's eagerness to register for the room and pay in advance, which was unnecessary (with a hundred-dollar bill), made Jacob apprehensive, as though he were being invaded—a sense that he dismissed as paranoia, to which he was also subject. But before he could sort out reactions, the young man had swung out of the driveway in his orange Datsun, presumably to fetch Valerie from the nearby hotel, which he had said they did not like. "So loud, you know?"

In fact, for no reason Jacob found that his heart was beating in jolts, so that quite out of character he went to the bar, unlocked it and poured himself a shot of brandy.

The bar, a narrow slat-roofed structure, was ten winding steps up from the pool, between the rental units and Jacob's own office-apartment-library. Curiously, it was almost never used by the Alaskan-North Dakotans, the young couples. Nor was the neat functional built-in barbecue, which was adjacent. Most of the units had kitchenettes, but still wouldn't they sometimes want to cook outside? The barbecue was the last "improvement" that Jacob had given to his resort. He had spent most of his earlier years in California, going from Los Angeles up to International House at Berkeley; he later concluded that he had been misled by that background; only Californians liked barbecues, and no one from California seemed to come his way.

Except for a disastrous visit from his best friend, fat Otto from I. House days, and Otto's new wife—a visit which Jacob had determined not to think about.

❧

The Datsun rushed back into the parking area, and "Valerie" got out. At first and somewhat distant glance, filtered through the bougainvillaea that hung about the bar, she was a delicately built young blonde. In dazzling white clothes. Huge dark glasses on a small face. An arrogant walk.

Jacob took a too large swallow of the rough brandy, which made him cough. So that both people turned to see him there at the bar, at eleven in the morning. ("You aroused *such* false expectations," Valerie said, later on.)

The young man, registered as Larry Cobb, waved, and Valerie smiled indefinitely. And a few minutes later, all the way from the room that he had rented them, Jacob heard a loud harsh voice that boomed, "But, darling, it's absolutely perfect."

Could that voice have come from such a delicate girl? He supposed it must. Jacob pulled on the large straw hat he always wore—he detested the sun—and hurried away from the bar.

❧

The practical or surface reason for Jacob's presence in this unlikely setting was that he had inherited it from his parents. However, as Otto had pointed out more than once, he could have sold it when they died, when the place was still in good shape. Now he'd have to spend God knows how much to fix it up—assuming, as Otto did assume, that he wanted to sell.

The Eisenmans had fled Berlin in the early Thirties, with their young son and a few remnants of their once-thriving rare-book business; following the terrible and familiarly circuitous route of the time (theirs had included Hong Kong), they finally reached Los Angeles, where they set up shop again and were (finally) successful enough to send their son to Berkeley. Later they were persuaded to invest in and retire to a warm island resort. It worked out well. They loved Kauai, where the sun warmed their tired bones and all around them magnificent flowers—flowers hitherto associated with expensive florists—effortlessly bloomed. Birds of paradise. Poinsettias, and of course everywhere the violent colors of bougainvillaea and hibiscus. They tended their property lovingly, and, a loving couple, they died peacefully within a week of each other. Jacob flew out to settle the estate and quixotically decided to stay. Well, why not? His Berkeley landlady could, and did, ship his books; besides, he was tired of graduate school, instructorships. And, as he wrote to Otto, "You know I have a horror of airplane flights. This way I avoid the return trip."

He promoted the woman who had been his parents' housekeeper to the position of manageress. Mrs. Wong, whom he then instructed to hire some local girls to help with the cleaning up. He was aware—his radar told him—that some of the local islanders imagined Mrs. Wong to be his mistress. He didn't mind; actually he liked her very much, but nothing could have been further from the truth.

Mrs. Wong was plain, round-faced, plump, and slovenly in her dress, and Jacob was sexually fastidious to the point of preferring celibacy to compromise. In fact in his entire life—he was almost fifty—he had had only three love affairs, and none of long duration; he was drawn to women who were violent, brilliant and intense, who were more than a little crazy. Crazy and extremely thin. "Basically I have a strong distaste for flesh," he had once confided to Otto.

"Which would explain your affection for myself." Otto had chuckled. "Pure masochism, of course."

Their kind of joke, in the good old lost days.

❧

"It was like labor pains," Valerie loudly and accusingly said; she was speaking of the waves that later that afternoon had knocked her to the sandy bottom of the ocean, and from which the young man, Larry, had

130

grabbed her out. "When Quentin was born, they kept coming back and back—"

She spoke furiously: why? From behind the bar where Jacob was making their drinks (he had never done this before, but the bar girl was sick and Mrs. Wong was somewhere else) he pondered her rage. At being a woman, forced painfully to bear children— blaming Larry for Quentin? No, they were not married; Larry certainly was not the father of Quentin, and she was not that silly. At Larry for having rescued her? No.

She was simply enraged at the sea for having knocked her down. It was an elemental rage, like Ahab's, which Jacob could admire; that was how he felt about the sun.

In the vine-filtered sunlight he could see that Valerie was older than he had thought, was somewhere in her thirties. All across her face, over the small nose, the slight rise of cheekbones, were tiny white tracings. Tiny scars. An exquisitely repaired face: Jacob did not want to imagine the accident involved, but then he did— driving too fast (in a convertible, it would have to have been a convertible) north of Boston, she had gone through a windshield. Her eyes were large and very dark, at first glance black, then perceived as an extraordinary midnight blue. Her voice was rasping, a whiskey voice, the accent crisply Bostonian. She was wearing something made of stiff white lace, through which a very small brown bikini was visible.

She gulped at her drink: straight gin, with a twist of lime. "God," she said, "I'm all scratched."

Larry asked her, "Does it hurt?"

"No, it just looks funny." She turned to Jacob. "You're so pale. Don't you go swimming at all?"

"No, I hate to swim."

She stared at him for an instant, and then seemed to understand a great deal at once; Jacob could literally feel her comprehension, which reached him like an affectionate hand.

She burst out laughing, a raucous, exhilarated laugh. "But that's absolutely marvelous!" she cried out. "I absolutely love it! You also hate the sun, right?"

Jacob nodded. But at the same time that he felt touched he also felt some part of his privacy invaded, which made him uneasy. He had been recognized.

"You must have a marvelous time here," said Larry, attempting a joke.

"I read a lot."

Larry did not like him.

"I need another drink," said Valerie, who probably had noted this too.

An impulse made Jacob say what he had not said before, to guests. "Look, I'm not always around. But if you want to drink that's where the key is," and he pointed to a spot at the top of a beam.

This was said to Larry (to make Larry like him better?), but it was Valerie who smiled and said, "That's really nice of you."

"We'll keep track" was what Larry said, and finally forgot to do.

Jacob left as soon as he could. He had decided to start rereading *Moby Dick*.

❧

Valerie liked his shabby place because she was rich, accustomed to grandeur. She was the opposite of upward ascendant: downward descendant? Was she that? Quite possible. Larry was somewhat younger than she, and rich in a different way: he had earned a lot of money, recently, in something trendy. A record company? TV? He resented Valerie's carelessness, her easy lack of ambitions.

Ahab said, "They think me mad, Starbuck does; but I'm demonic, I am madness maddened! that wild madness that's only calm to comprehend itself—"

⇜⥁⇝

Valerie had (probably) been married several times. Perhaps a husband had been with her when she smashed up the car? A now dead husband?

⇜⥁⇝

At about eleven the next morning, when Jacob approached the bar, Valerie was perched on a high stool, her long thin brown legs drawn up childishly. She had made herself a tall drink. "Won't you join me?"

"I don't drink much—no, thanks." Then, to her raised eyebrows, he added, "Yesterday was out of character."

"You aroused *such* false expectations." She let that go, and then asked, as though it were what they had been talking about for some time, "How do you feel about flying?"

"I hate it. That's one reason I'm here."

In an instant she had taken that in, and her riotous laugh broke out. "That's terrific!" Then she said, "But what do you do about it?"

"Obviously: I don't fly."

"If I could only understand why I'm so afraid. Larry has driven off to Koloa," she added, irrelevantly. "You'd think I'd be afraid to drive." And she told him then about her accident, the crashed convertible in which her second husband had been killed, the crash that in some sense he had already seen.

Jacob understood that they were communicating on levels that he could not fathom, that even made him

133

somewhat uncomfortable. He could so vividly see and feel whatever she told him; apparently, in fact, even before she spoke.

"I have some idiot faith that if I could understand it I wouldn't be afraid anymore. Of flying," Valerie said. "I think that's what's called shrink-conditioning. I've even tried to 'associate' to the fear, and I do remember something weird: myself, but in a white wicker carriage, a *baby* carriage—how could I remember *that?* Anyway my nurse is pushing it, a young Irish girl. And we're at the top of a hill in Magnolia, near the shore, and some older kids tell her to let it go—"

But she might as well have stopped talking, because Jacob could see it: a stoned-fenced New England landscape, wild roses. A pretty dark maid with a tweed coat pulled over a white uniform. "But she didn't let go," he gently said.

"Of course not. But what in hell does that have to do with being afraid to fly?"

❦

Larry arranged to go deep-sea fishing, near Lihue. Valerie sat by the pool, in a white bikini, with a stack of books. Seeing her there from above, as he conferred with Mrs. Wong about the necessity for a second visit from the plumber, Jacob was aware that he could go down to her and pull up a chair; they could talk all day. But that prospect was too much for him; it made his heart race. Instead he went back to the dim seclusion of his library; he went from *Moby Dick* to Nerval, *"Je suis le Ténébreux—le Veuf—"* He went out into the sunlight.

He and Valerie had a brief conversation about Jane Austen, whom she was rereading. "I read her to regain some balance," said Valerie.

"You might try reading her on planes."

She gave him a long speculative look. "What a good idea."

Pretending busyness, Jacob went back to his office.

In fact all that day was punctuated with such brief conversations. Her nondemanding cool friendliness, her independence made this possible; they matched, or supplemented, his vast diffidence.

She asked, "How is it around Hanalei, the northern coast?"

"I don't know. I've never been there."

"You're absolutely marvelous."

"Do you think it's a fear that someone will throw you out of the sky—like God?"

"Alas, poor Icarus."

"Yes, that's sort of it. As though you shouldn't be up there, so high."

Sometime in the midafternoon he found her at the bar with a long drink.

"You know what I really like about this place?" she asked. "The whales. They're terrific, spouting out there."

"Yes." Her tan intensified the whiteness of her scars, making a sort of jigsaw of her face. Her eyes were dark and wild, and after a little while Jacob realized that she was drunk, or nearly so: like most people, he had trouble recognizing conditions foreign to himself. It had taken him a long time to see that Otto's wife,

Joanne, was very stupid; at first he had thought her crazy, which was something he knew more about. In fact she was both.

He said, "A long time ago a woman came here who hated the whales, she was terrified of them."

"*Really?*" Valerie leaned forward, toward his face so that he caught a whiff of exotic perfume, of musk.

"It finally turned out that she had them confused with sharks, and thought they would swim in and bite her."

"Good Christ."

"She was exceptionally stupid. My best friend's wife."

The first surprise had been Otto's extreme prosperity, as evidenced by the casual mention of buying several condominiums, on the peninsula south of San Francisco. "Well, I have to have them for tax shelters." In fact he had come to Hawaii to talk to a group of businessmen in Honolulu who were interested in some California coastal property. Not to see Jacob. The second surprise (probably not wholly unconnected with the first) was Joanne. Joanne from San Antonio, with her raven hair and milk-white skin, her rosebud mouth. (Otto's taste in women had never been original.) Big girlish breasts. A tiny well-focused mind. "Oh, I just think you're so *smart* not to waste your money on paint and fixing things up. I mean, who'd care?" And, "Oh, I just love all these darling yellow-brown people; they don't look a bit like darkies." Over her head Jacob had at first sought Otto's eyes, but Otto wasn't listening; in fact he had never (Jacob remembered too late) enjoyed talking or listening to women; he probably didn't hear a word she said. But Jacob heard it all, each abrasive idiocy, delivered in that nasal soprano. "Those are

136

really whales out there? But how does anybody dare to go in swimming?"

One curious—to Jacob, incomprehensible—facet of Joanne's character was her imperviousness to coldness on another's part, to slights. Not that Jacob really slighted her, but surely his politeness came across coldly? Actually he couldn't stand her, and he found it hard to pretend otherwise. But she continued her bubbling smiles and winks (Christ, *winks!*) at him; on any pretext at all she stood so close that her glossy head touched his shoulder; she would introduce a sentence by touching his arm. Incredible! Jacob considered, and instantly dismissed, the insane possibility that she was sexually drawn to him; modesty aside, he found that unlikely. He had none of the qualities that would have drawn her to Otto, for example; he was not rich or ebullient or pleasure-loving (God knows, not that). Also he was bony, his dry skin was deeply lined, whereas Otto was sleek and fat. No, he decided, she was simply behaving as she always did with men.

Such was his estimate of Joanne, and of their situation up to the final terrible night of which he would not think: the knock at his door. (He had somehow known it was Joanne, and had frighteningly thought that Otto must be sick.) But, "You can't imagine how sound your old friend sleeps," she had said, pushing past him in her frilly thigh-length gown, beneath which unleashed fat breasts bounced. "I thought we could have a tiny drinkie together," she said. "I just feel as though I hardly know you at all." Her young face shone with joyous self-adulation.

Jacob couldn't believe it, not then or later (now) remembering. How had he got rid of her? He had muttered something about a strep throat, clutching at his neck. An insane impulse that had worked: Joanne was terrified of germs.

Most men of course would not have sent her away,

and so friendship dictated that Jacob inform Otto. "You are married to a sub-moronic nymphomaniac. Even if you don't listen to her conversation. She is a bad person. She will do you harm." Of course the next day he said nothing of the sort, and for all Jacob knew Otto and Joanne were what is known as "happily married." Otto rarely mentioned her in his letters.

"One encouraging thing I recently read," said Valerie, beginning to slur a little, "is that if you fall from more than six thousand feet—or was it sixty thousand?—you die of a heart attack before you hit the ground. If you call that encouraging."

"I suppose you could."

"Well, I do. Christ, I'm sleepy. I'm going in for a nap."

She walked off unsteadily, between the clamorously brilliant blooms. Jacob heard the slam of her screen door.

That night, as he restlessly rebegan *The Wanderer* (he was slipping from book to book, a familiar bad sign), Jacob could hear them at the barbecue (it's first use); in fact he could smell their steak. Valerie and Larry. Her rowdy laugh, his neat clipped voice.

Then it turned into a quarrel; Jacob caught the tone but not the words. Very quietly he got up and opened his door. Without a sound he went out, walking away from them through the dark until he could hear nothing at all. Down the small road, past all the oversized blooming plants, he walked, toward the small arc of beach, the surfers' beach, now coldly gray-white in the dark. There he stood on the mound of black lava rock, regarding the shining waves, their wicked curl before breaking, until one huge wave—as large, he imagined, as a giant whale—crashed near his rock and drove him back, and he started home. As he reached his door everything was still, no voices from the bar or anywhere. Only surf.

❧

He didn't see Valerie (or Larry) all the next day until late afternoon when together they approached the bar, where Jacob had been talking to his liquor supplier, Mr. Mederious; he had needed to order more gin. Valerie and Larry were merry, friendly with each other, holding hands. Sand dried in their uncombed hair, his so dark, hers pale.

"We found the most fabulous beach—"

"—absolutely private, no one there at all."

"—really beautiful."

They had made love on the beach.

"I could stay here forever," said Valerie, dreamily.

"Baby, some of us have to work," Larry said, with some affection. But of course this was an issue between them. Also, Larry would have liked to marry her, and she didn't want to get married, having done it so often before.

Jacob knew everything.

❧

Re-embarked on his own Jane Austen, he found that at last he was able to concentrate. He spent the next few days alone with *Emma, Persuasion, Northanger Abbey*—pure delight, a shining impeccable world, like Mozart, Flemish painting.

When next he saw Valerie, in still another bikini— beside the pool, Larry had gone fishing again—she was

139

even browner. She looked clear-eyed, younger. "When we were in Honolulu," she told Jacob, "we saw the most amazing man on the sidewalk. Dressed in red, white and blue striped clothes, with an Uncle Sam hat. And sandwich boards with really crazy things written on them. Peace sign labeled 'Chicken Tracks of a Coward.' Something about abortion is murder. Really extraordinary—the superpatriot. I could not figure out what he was about."

Of course Jacob could see the man. Hunched over, lost.

"You know," she said, "I've got to get into some kind of work." Her harsh laugh. "I might even try to finish school. Last time around I got married instead."

"I think you should."

She laughed again. "Larry will die."

"He will?"

"He's not strong on intellectual women."

❧❀❧

One night, as Jacob lay half asleep on his narrow hard bed (his monk's bed, as he thought of it), he heard what he imagined to be a knock on his door. At first he thought, Good Christ, Joanne? But of course Joanne was nowhere near, and his heart leaped up as he reached for the ancient canvas trench coat that served him as a robe, and he went to open the door.

No one there. But had there been?

He stood still in the starry flowering night, listening for any sound.

Someone was at the bar, and he walked in that direction.

Valerie. And at the instant that he saw her he also saw and heard the orange Datsun start up and swing out of the driveway, into the sleeping night.

Valerie, in a tailored red silk robe, was applying ice

cubes to one eye, ice cubes neatly wrapped in a paper napkin; her performance was expert, practiced. She said, "You catch me at a disadvantage. I seem to have walked into the proverbial door."

"Can I—" He was not sure what he had meant to offer.

"No, I'll be all right. Care for a drink?"

She already had one, something dark on ice.

Jacob poured himself a shot of brandy.

She said, "You know, it's too bad that children are brought up so much with globes for toys. They see the world as a small ball full of oceans, with those insecure patches of land."

She spoke with great intensity, her visible dark eye huge. She was not drunk but Jacob sensed that earlier she had been. He wanted to ask her if she had, in fact, knocked on his door.

She said, "Tonight I was thinking about those old globes, and how these islands look on them, and I thought we might fall off into space. Do you think I'm going crazy?"

"No, I don't."

"God, I may never get back on a plane."

Jacob wanted to say, Don't. Don't go anywhere, stay with me. Read all my books, and then I'll send for more. Talk to me when you want to. Stay.

Valerie stood up, stretching. She still kept the side of her face that must by now be swollen and discolored turned away. She said, "Well, I think I can sleep now. See you in the morning."

In the morning he could say to her what he had meant to say.

Jacob went off to bed and while he was still reading (impossible then to sleep) he heard the Datsun return. Stop. Slam.

In the morning Valerie and Larry came to Jacob's office together, both dressed for travel—she in dark-blue linen, huge glasses covering whatever had happened to her eye, Larry in pale gray.

They had simply and suddenly decided to leave. They felt that they had to get back. Larry's new TV show. Quentin.

Jacob and Valerie shook hands—their only touch. Her hand was small and hard and strong, and she wore a lot of rings. "I'm absolutely terrified," she said, with a beautiful quick smile. "All those flights."

Jacob said, "You'll be all right," and he smiled too. Goodbye.

But he was not at all sure of what he said. All that day he was terrified of her flights.

Beautiful Girl

Ardis Bascombe, the tobacco heiress, who twenty years ago was a North Carolina beauty queen, is now sitting in the kitchen of her San Francisco house, getting drunk. Four-thirty, an October afternoon, and Ardis, with a glass full of vodka and melted ice, a long cigarette going and another smoldering in an almost full ashtray, is actually doing several things at once: drinking and smoking, of course, killing herself, her older daughter, Linda, has said (Ardis is no longer speaking to Linda, who owns and runs a health-food store), and watching the news on her small color Sony TV. She is waiting for her younger daughter, Carrie, who goes to Stanford but lives at home and usually shows up about now. And she is waiting also for a guest, a man she knew way back when, who called this morning, whose name she is having trouble with. Black? White? Green? It is a color name; she is sure of that.

Twenty years ago Ardis was a small and slender black-haired girl, with amazing wide, thickly lashed dark-azure eyes and smooth, pale, almost translucent skin—a classic Southern beauty, except for the sexily curled, contemptuous mouth. And brilliant, too: straight A's at Chapel Hill. An infinitely promising, rarely lovely girl: everyone thought so. A large portrait of her then hangs framed on the kitchen wall: bare-shouldered, in something gauzy, light—she is dressed for a formal dance, the Winter Germans or the May Frolics. The portrait is flyspecked and streaked with grime from the kitchen fumes. Ardis despises cleaning up, and hates having maids around; periodically she calls a janitorial service, and sometimes she has various rooms repainted, covering the grime. Nevertheless, the picture shows the face of a beautiful young girl. Also hanging there, gilt-framed and similarly grimed, are several family portraits; elegant and upright ancestors, attesting to family substance—although in Ardis's messy kitchen they have a slightly comic look of inappropriateness.

Ardis's daughter Carrie, who in a couple of years will inherit several of those tobacco millions, is now driving up from the peninsula, toward home, in her jaunty brown felt hat and patched fadded jeans, in her dirty battered Ford pickup truck. She is trying to concentrate on Thomas Jefferson (History I) or the view: blond subdivided hills and groves of rattling dusty eucalyptus trees that smell like cat pee. She is listening to the conversations on her CB radio, but a vision of her mother, at the table, with her emptying glass and heavy blue aura of smoke, fills Carrie's mind; she is pervaded by the prospect of her mother and filled with guilt, apprehension, sympathy. Her mother, who used to be so much fun, now looks as swollen and dead-eyed, as thick-skinned, as a frog.

Hoping for change, Carrie has continued to live at home, seldom admitting why. Her older sister, Linda, of the health-food store, is more severe, or simply fatalistic. "If she wants to drink herself to death she will," says Linda. "Your being there won't help, or change a thing." Of course she's right, but Carrie sticks around.

Neither Linda nor Carrie is as lovely as their mother was. They are pretty girls—especially Linda, who is snub-nosed and curly-haired. Carrie has straight dark hair and a nose like that of her father: Clayton Bascombe, former Carolina Deke, former tennis star, former husband of Ardis. His was a nice straight nose—Clayton was an exceptionally handsome boy—but it is too long now for Carrie's small tender face.

Clayton, too, had a look of innocence; perhaps it was his innocent look that originally attracted Ardis's strong instinct for destruction. In any case, after four years of marriage, two daughters, Ardis decided that Clayton was "impossible," and threw him out—out of the house that her parents had given them, in Winston-Salem. Now Clayton is in real estate in Wilmington, N.C., having ended up where he began, before college and the adventure of marriage to Ardis.

Ardis has never remarried. For many years, in Winston-Salem, as a young divorcée, she was giddily popular, off to as many parties and weekends out of town as when she was a Carolina coed. Then, after the end of an especially violent love affair, she announced that she was tired of all that and bored with all her friends. With the two girls, Ardis moved to San Francisco, bought the big house on Vallejo Street, had it fashionably decorated and began another round of parties with new people—a hectic pace that gradually slowed to fewer parties, invitations, friends. People became "boring" or "impossible," as the neglected house decayed. Ardis spent more and more time alone. More time drunk.

The girls, who from childhood had been used to their mother's lovers (suitors, beaux) and who by now had some of their own, were at first quite puzzled by their absence: Ardis, without men around? Then Linda said to Carrie, "Well, *Lord,* who'd want her now? Look at that face. Besides, I think she'd rather drink."

In some ways Ardis has been a wonderful mother, though: Carrie sometimes says that to herself. Always there were terrific birthday parties, presents, clothes. And there was the time in Winston-Salem when the real-estate woman came to the door with a petition about Negroes—keeping them out, land values, something like that. Of course Ardis refused to sign, and then she went on: "And in answer to your next question, I sincerely hope that both my daughters marry them. I understand those guys are really great. *Not,* unfortunately, from personal experience." *Well.* What other mother, especially in Winston-Salem, would ever talk like that?

❧

Ardis dislikes paying bills—especially small ones; for instance, from the garbage collectors, although she loves their names. Sunset Scavenger Company. Thus the parking area is lined with full garbage cans, spilling over among all the expensively imported and dying rhododendrons and magnolia trees, the already dead azaleas in their rusted cans. Seeing none of this, Carrie parks her truck. She gets out and slams the door.

Five o'clock. Ardis will have had enough drinks to make her want to talk a lot, although she will be just beginning to not make sense.

Carrie opens the front door and goes in, and she hears her mother's familiar raucous laugh coming from the kitchen. Good, she is not alone. Carrie walks in that direction, as Ardis's deep, hoarse voice explains to someone, "That must be my daughter Carrie. You won't believe—"

Carrie goes into the kitchen and is introduced to a tall, thin, almost bald, large-nosed man. He is about

146

her mother's age but in much better shape: rich, successful. (Having inherited some of her mother's social antennae, Carrie has taken all this in without really thinking.) In Ardis's dignified slur, his name sounds like Wopple Grin.

❧§❧

"Actually," Ardis tells Carrie later on, "Walpole Greene is very important in Washington, on the Hill." This has been said in the heavily nasal accent with which Ardis imitates extreme snobs; like many good mimics, she is aping an unacknowledged part of herself. Ardis is more truly snobbish than anyone, caring deeply about money, family and position. "Although he certainly wasn't much at Carolina," she goes on, in the same tone.

Tonight, Ardis looks a little better than usual, her daughter observes. She did a very good job with her makeup; somehow her eyes look O.K.—not as popped out as they sometimes do. And a gauzy scarf around her throat has made it look less swollen.

Walpole Greene, who is indeed important in Washington, although, as the head of a news bureau, not exactly in Ardis's sense "on the Hill," thinks how odd it is that Ardis should have such a funny-looking kid.

Carrie, reading some of that in his face, thinks, What a creep. She excuses herself to go upstairs. She smiles privately as she leaves, repeating, silently, "Wopple Grin."

❧§❧

In Chapel Hill, all those years ago, in the days when Walpole Greene was certainly not much—he was too young, too skinny and tall; with his big nose he looked like a bird—he was always acutely and enragedly aware

147

of Ardis. So small and bright, so admired, so universally lusted after, so often photographed in the *Daily Tarheel* and *Carolina Magazine,* with her half-inviting, half-disdainful smile; she was everywhere. One summer, during a session of summer school, Walpole felt that he saw Ardis every time he left his dorm: Ardis saying "Hey, Walpole" (Wopple? was she teasing him?) in the same voice in which she said "Hey" to everyone.

He saw her dancing in front of the Y, between classes, in the morning—smiling, mocking the dance. He glimpsed her through the windows of Harry's, drinking beer, in the late afternoon. She was dressed always in immaculate pale clothes: flowered cottons, cashmere cardigans. And at night he would see her anywhere at all: coming out of the show, at record concerts in Kenan Stadium ("Music Under the Stars"), emerging from the Arboretum, with some guy. Usually she was laughing, which made even then a surprisingly loud noise from such a small thin girl. Her laugh and her walk were out of scale; she *strode,* like someone very tall and important.

Keeping track of her, Walpole, who had an orderly mind, began to observe a curious pattern in the escorts of Ardis: midmornings at the Y, evenings at the show, or at Harry's, she was apt to be with Gifford Gwathmey, a well-known S.A.E., a handsome blond Southern boy. But if he saw her in some more dubious place, like the Arboretum, late at night, she would be with Henry Mallory, a Delta Psi from Philadelphia.

Ardis always looked as if she were at a party, having a very good time but at the same time observing carefully and feeling just slightly superior to it all. And since his sense of himself and of his presence at Carolina was precisely opposite to that, Walpole sometimes dreamed of doing violence to Ardis. He hated her almost as much as he hated the dean of men, who in a conference had suggested that Walpole should "get out more," should "try to mix in."

It was a melancholy time for Walpole, all around.

One August night, in a stronger than usual mood of self-pity, Walpole determined to do what he had all summer considered doing: he would stay up all night and then go out to Gimghoul Castle (the Gimghouls were an undergraduate secret society) and watch the dawn from the lookout bench there. He did just that, drinking coffee and reading from *The Federalist Papers,* and then riding on his bike, past the Arboretum and Battle Park, to the Castle. The lookout bench was some distance from the main building, as he approached it Walpole noted that a group of people, probably Gimghouls and their dates, were out there drinking *still,* on one of the terraces.

He settled on the hard stone circular bench, in the dewy pre-dawn air, and focused his attention on the eastern horizon. And then suddenly, soundlessly—and drunkenly: she was plastered—Ardis appeared. Weaving toward him, she sat down on the bench beside him, though not too near.

"You came out here to look at the sunrise?" she slurred, conversationally. "God, Wopple, that's wonderful." Wunnerful.

Tears of hatred sprang to Walpole's eyes—fortunately invisible. He choked; in a minute he would hit her, very hard.

Unaware that she was in danger, Ardis got stiffly to her feet; she bent awkwardly toward him and placed a cool bourbon-tasting kiss on Walpole's mouth. "I love you, Wopple," Ardis said. "I truly and purely do." The sun came up.

He didn't hate her anymore—of course he would not hit her. How could he hit a girl who had kissed him and spoken of love? And although after that night nothing between them changed overtly, he now watched her as a lover would. With love.

❧❧❧

"Lord, you're lucky I didn't rape you there and then," says Ardis now, having heard this romantic story. She is exaggerating the slur of her speech, imitating someone even drunker than she is.

Walpole, who believes that in a way he has loved her all his life, laughs sadly, and he wonders if at any point in her life Ardis could have been—he backs off from "saved" and settles on "retrieved." Such a waste: such beauty gone, and brains and wit. Walpole himself has just married again, for the fourth time: a young woman who, he has already begun to recognize, is not very nice, or bright. He has little luck with love. It is not necessarily true that Ardis would have been better off with him.

She is clearly in no shape to go out to dinner, and Walpole wonders if he shouldn't cook something for the two of them to eat. Scrambled eggs? He looks around the impossibly disordered kitchen, at stacks of dishes, piled-up newspapers, a smelly cat box in one corner, although he has seen no cat.

He reaches and pours some more vodka into his own glass, then glances over at Ardis, whose eyes have begun to close.

By way of testing her, he asks, "Something I always wondered. That summer, I used to see you around with Gifford Gwathmey, and then later you'd be with Henry Mallory. Weren't you pinned to Gifford?"

Ardis abruptly comes awake, and emits her laugh. "Of course I was pinned to Giff," she chortles. "But he and all those S.A.E.s were almost as boring as Dekes, although he did come from one of the oldest and *richest*

150

families in Charleston." (This last in her nasal snob-imitating voice.) "So I used to late-date on him all the time, mainly with Henry, who didn't have a dime. But the Delta Psis were *fun*—they had *style*—a lot of boys from New York and Philadelphia." She laughs again. "Between dates, I'd rush back to the House and brush my teeth—talk about your basic fastidious coed. Henry teased me about always tasting of Pepsodent." For a moment Ardis looks extremely happy, and almost young; then she falls slowly forward until her head rests on the table in front of her, and she begins to snore.

❦

Carrie, who has recently discovered jazz, is upstairs listening to old Louis Armstrong records, smoking a joint. "Pale moon shining on the fields below . . ."

She is thinking, as she often does, of how much she would like to get out of this house for a while. She would like to drop out of school for a term or two, maybe next spring, and just get into her truck with a few clothes and some money, and maybe a dog, and drive around the country. There is a huge circular route that she has often imagined: up to Seattle, maybe Canada, Vancouver, down into Wyoming, across the northern plains to Chicago—she knows someone there—New England, New York and down the coast to her father, in Wilmington, N.C.; Charleston, New Orleans, Texas, Mexico, the Southwest, L.A.; then home, by way of Big Sur. Months of driving, with the dog and the CB radio for company.

In the meantime, halfway through her second joint, she sighs deeply and realizes that she is extremely hungry, ravenous. She carefully stubs out the joint and goes downstairs.

Walpole Greene, whose presence she had forgotten, is standing in the pantry, looking lost. Ardis has passed out. Having also forgotten that she thought he was a creep, Carrie experiences a rush of sympathy for the poor guy. "Don't worry," she tells him. "She'll be O.K."

"She sure as hell doesn't look O.K.," says Walpole Greene. "She's not O.K. No one who drinks that much—"

"Oh, well, in the long run you're right," says Carrie, as airily as though she had never worried about her mother's health. "But I mean for now she's O.K."

"Well. I'd meant to take her out to dinner."

"Why bother? She doesn't eat. But aren't you hungry? I'm starved."

"Well, sort of." Walpole looks dubiously around the kitchen. He watches Carrie as she goes over to the mammoth refrigerator and extracts a small covered saucepan from its incredibly crowded, murky interior.

"She likes to make soup," says Carrie. "Lately she's been on some Southern kick. Nostalgia, I guess. This is white beans and pork. Just made yesterday, so it ought to be all right."

The soup, which Carrie has heated and ladled into bowls, is good but too spicy for Walpole's ulcer; the next day he will feel really terrible. Now he and Carrie whisper to each other, like conspirators, above the sound of Ardis's heavy breathing.

"Does she do this often?" asks Walpole.

"Pretty often. Well—like, every day."

"That's not good."

"No."

Having drunk quite a bit more than he usually does, Walpole feels that his perceptions are enlarged. Looking at Carrie, he has a sudden and certain vision of her future: in ten or so years, in her late twenties, early thirties, she will be more beautiful than even Ardis ever was. She will be an exceptional beauty, a beautiful woman, whereas Ardis was just a beautiful girl. Should he tell Carrie that? He decides not to; she wouldn't believe him, although he is absolutely sure of his perception. Besides, even a little drunk he is too shy.

Instead, in an inspired burst, he says, "Listen, she's got to go somewhere. You know, dry out. There's a place in Connecticut. Senators' wives—"

Carrie's bright young eyes shine, beautifully. "That would be neat," she says.

"You'd be O.K. by yourself for a while?"

"I really would. I'm thinking about getting a dog— our cat just disappeared. And there's this trip. But how would you get her there?"

"Leave that to me," says Walpole, with somewhat dizzy confidence.

Carrie clears the table—without, Walpole notices, washing any dishes.

❧❧❧

Carrie goes back upstairs, her heart high and light.

She considers calling her sister, Linda, saying that Walpole Greene is taking their mother to Connecticut. But Linda would say something negative, unpleasant.

Instead, she puts on another record, and hears the rich pure liquid sound of Louis's horn, and then his voice. "Beale Street Blues," "Muskrat Ramble," "A Son of the South." She listens, blows more joints.

❧❧❧

Downstairs, seated at the table, Walpole is talking softly and persuasively, he hopes, to Ardis's ear (her small pink ears are still pretty, he has noticed), although she is "asleep."

"This lovely place in Connecticut," he is saying. "A

wonderful place. You'll like it. You'll rest, and eat good food, and you'll feel better than you've felt for years. You'll see. I want you to be my beautiful girl again—"

Suddenly aroused, Ardis raises her head and stares at Walpole. "I am a beautiful girl," she rasps out, furiously.

Home Is Where

In San Francisco there is apt to be no spring at all. During one such season of grayness, cold and wind, when everything else in my life was also terrible, I felt that I would die of longing for home—"home" being in my case a small Southern river town, not far inland from the Atlantic coast.

My problems were more serious than I could cope with or even think about: a husband, a lover and a landlady, all of whom I was terrified of, and a son for whose future, in those conditions, I greatly feared. And so, instead, I thought about hot river smells, jasmine and hyacinth and gardenias, caves of honeysuckle and live oaks festooned with Spanish moss.

And finally, in June (there was still no summer, no remission of cold and fog), against some better judgment, with my son I rushed back there—rushed toward what, in another frame of mind, I might have considered an origin of my troubles: alcoholic parents, a disapproving, narrow small town that still (probably) contained several former lovers (I had been a wild young girl) and some inimical former friends.

Exhilarated by a remembrance of steamy river

afternoons, canoe trips down to small white beaches and summer night dances, I went and bought some light new clothes—cotton shorts, flouncy pastel dresses—such as out in San Francisco I hadn't needed for years. My married life had made me feel ugly—drained and discolored, old; and with the unerringly poor judgment of a depressed person I had found a lover who disliked me, who in fact was a little crazy, mean. Perhaps as much as anything else I needed to return to a place where I had been young and, if never beautiful, at least sought after.

And once my plans were made, my problems seemed somewhat to abate: the landlady herself went away on vacation, so that for a time there were no more of those harrowing, repeated phone calls about the noise of my son's running footsteps (Simon, at four, not a heavy or clumsy child); my lover was sympathetic (possibly relieved, since we had chosen each other out of angry needs?); my husband took Simon and me out for a pleasant, noncritical parting dinner, at a good Italian restaurant. He only said, "You won't be eating food like this for a while, will you, Claire," and I said that I supposed not.

Perhaps I did not have to go home after all? But by then I was committed. Letters written, tickets bought. And those clothes.

Only on the plane did some of the drawbacks inherent in my plan occur to me: my selfish parents' total indifference to children; the extreme heat, to which neither Simon nor I (now) was used; and the embarrassment (fear) of seeing certain people there—Mary Sue, my girlhood rival-friend-enemy; Dudley Farmer, with whom I had once had a violent and badly ending love; other friends.

And so I flew across the country in a wild mixture of fear and excitement, a state that was all too familiar to me: it was how I felt on getting married (rightly, as things turned out); how I felt each time I went to meet my lover. Often, when the phone rang I was afraid.

My apprehensive state increased in Washington—Kennedy Airport, where we were to change planes to go south, to go home. And by the time we were on that second plane, heading up through small puffy clouds in a pastel-blue sky, I was babbling to Simon, crazily: "Remind me to show you—take you—tell you about—"

He was fine, so far. Filled, perhaps, with nice kindergarten stories about little boys going to visit their grandparents, my volatile, difficult, demanding and adored young son sat buckled into his seat in seeming contentment. He listened to the ravings of his mother, himself at peace, sipping his diet cola (ludicrous, such a tall thin child, but having failed him in large ways I have tended to yield on small issues). I gulped vodka.

The plane landed and skidded along a red clay field—my part of the South is made almost entirely of red clay; the rest is dust. And we headed toward a one-story white clapboard building, the terminal. In front there was a high wire fence, next to which stood a portly, white-haired, red-faced man, very erect, in a white linen suit: my father. I would of course have known him anywhere, picked him out in any crowd, but what I first thought was: Oh! I'd forgotten how short he is. By reasonable standards he is not short, almost six feet, but I had been involved with unreasonably tall men: my husband, six two, and my lover, an impossible six four. My son too will be very tall.

We got out, Simon and I holding hands down the steps; for an instant I felt my father's eyes pass across and not recognize us. But then he did, and we were all upon each other, embracing and saying familiar blank words and smelling familiar smells: his cigarette-smoked clothes and breath, shaving lotion and mint (mints to kill the smell of bourbon). I don't know what about me seemed or smelled familiar: I switch perfumes a lot and drink scentless vodka—or Simon, whom he had only seen two or three times before, at widely spaced intervals.

Another thing I had forgotten about my father: he is impossible to understand until you have been with him for several days. He has a heavy Southern accent and he speaks extremely fast, generally with a cigarette in his mouth. And so, as we drove over the long flat white miles toward home, over swamps, past creeks and dried-out rutted farmland where the only shade was a single chinaberry tree, we did not exactly have a conversation. I said that my husband was fine but working too hard—"you know how he is" (which my father did not know). I didn't mention trouble with the landlady and certainly not my dangerous lover.

Between us, forgotten by us both, Simon sat forward on his seat and stared at everything.

As we approached our town, "New hospital!" my father cried out triumphantly, and he pointed toward a towering white mass of concrete and glass and steel that rose unrelatedly from a spreading pine grove. Its busy parking lot was islanded with buckets of thin young trees; the landscaping confirmed the newness of the place—to me it all looked raw and hostile. And so large: I had a quick image of all the inhabitants of our small town being sucked inside.

Just then my father was saying something about Dudley Farmer (I thought) and then (surely unconnectedly)—"psychoanalyst, from Boston, Harvard College, I believe, doing some sort of research—" but I really couldn't hear this either.

When we got to the house—a big, pillared box, imposingly back from the river—the sun was still high, yellow-hazed above the brown slow water, but actually it was five o'clock. "Time for a drink!" said my father, as he did each day at that time.

I was suddenly exhausted, and strangely inwardly tearful: a drink seemed a good idea. My mother was still asleep; she spends the afternoon sleeping off the lunchtime sherry, and then it's time to start again. And so we sat on the porch and waited for her entrance, while Simon ran down to the dock, where he took off his shoes and waded at the shallow muddy river edge.

My father was going on about the wonderful new hospital, the gift of a prominent (and dreadful right-wing rich red-neck, I thought) local family, and he mentioned again, with one of his curious jolting laughs, the psychoanalyst who had come down from Boston to do some work in the hospital, research. ("Artistic Negro children" is what my father said; I later learned he meant autistic—in his accent, impossible to tell.) And in a dreamy bleary way I thought, Good, I will have a summer romance with the Boston shrink. God knows I could use one, or both.

My mother is one of those women who, having been great beauties, forever retain that air; automatically people defer to and wait on her. All my life I had watched her performances with a defeated, angry envy, as I too deferred and waited on her. It was hard to believe that we belonged to the same sex, much less the same family. Now she came in, scarves floating around that faded golden head; my father and I stood up and she kissed us both, and we started getting things for her: a special drink, an ashtray and then another scarf that she had left upstairs in her bedroom.

I told her that I was fine, that it was good to be home. That she looked wonderful.

"Did Daddy tell you about poor Dudley Farmer?" she asked me next. "Has to have this terrible operation on his stomach, they say they're going to take out most of it. He's scared, I tell you. Supposed to lose a lot of weight."

"Is Dudley fat?" This seemed incredible: Dudley had

been tall and lithe, a basketball star, with severe dark-blue eyes and an ironic mouth.

"Oh, very fat, you wouldn't recognize him, not any way. Got fat because of his ulcers, and now they have to operate."

The sun was lowering now; I watched it set over the river, as I had thousands of times before (but had it ever set into just those violet clouds, that pink?). And I thought, Oh, the strangeness of the intensely familiar, the wild confusions involved in coming home! It was truly as though I had never left, and at the same time as though I were a stranger, new to that place and to those people, my parents.

Forgetting Simon (as I'm sure they often forgot about me, at his age), they were getting a little drunk as we sat there in the barely cooling air, among fireflies and flowery smells from the shrubbery—until Simon came running up and said he was hungry. The maid had gone home—my parents were "good to the help"—and so my unmaternal mother said, "Why don't you go and see what's in the icebox?" just as she used to say to me, making me feel lonely and neglected. But Simon thought this was great—was freedom: no cross father telling him to eat his meat *first*. He came back after a while with an unbelievably messy sandwich, which looked to be made of chicken and peanut butter and chutney, which he had put together all by himself—and no one forced him to eat it.

The rest of us skipped dinner. I ate a hard-boiled egg on the way to bed, and slept hungrily, with agonizing dreams; I probably wept.

And the next day I fell in love with the Boston doctor.

Or, rather, the next afternoon. That morning, clutching Simon by the hand, wearing my new white shorts and hiding behind very large dark glasses, I wandered through the town—invisible.

The main street of our town is like that of so many small Southern towns: tacky, tawdry, unchanging. The Chatham Dairy Products, to which all of us in high school used to rush each afternoon, to pile around those tables, eating sundaes out of Dixie Cups, showing off for each other—the boys being funny, the girls laughing.

The Little Athens: a dark and dirty beer parlor, with high rickety curtained booths, where Dudley and I often began our evenings, began to kiss and grasp at each other, before we rushed out to his car, rushed down the highway to our small private clearing in a thicket of honeysuckle and crape myrtle, parked. (Adolescent sex, or, usually, non- or almost-sex: what a ghastly preparation for anything! How can anyone romanticize it? How can I?) Until Dudley dumped me and took up with Mary Sue, and then dumped her for a young married woman in another town.

❧

Adolescent memories are not only the most recent and thus the most available, they are also the least subtle, the simplest. Below them stretch deeper, darker layers. However, instead of telling Simon about the time I lost my nickel on the way to Sunday school and hid under the giant magnolia tree (that one, *there*) feeling criminal, I took him to the dime store, where we bought two toy boats and a shovel and pail, and then we continued to the A&P, with my mother's shopping list—to which I added a pound of hamburger; I had decided on certain precautions against skipping dinner.

After that, since the groceries were to be delivered, we walked some more, Simon noticing and asking questions about things, as I remembered everything that had ever happened to me, my whole past assailing me like light continuously thrown stones.

❧

Lunch, naps—for my half-drunk parents, my exhausted son. My father had muttered (I could still barely understand him) that the Boston doctor might come by with a book, and so I sat down out on the porch with a book of my own in my lap, in my short white shorts, in the glaring yellow afternoon sun. Waiting.

After a while I heard a car pull into our drive, behind the house; from the creaking sound of it, a very old car. (A doctor, with an old car? I thought, Terrific.) I heard the engine cut off, a door slam; I saw a tall man come around the corner. A man whom I got up and walked down the steps to greet.

Love at first sight is a silly feeling on one's face: standing there in the heavy sunlight, near a clump of hydrangeas, I looked up at his craggy reddish face, with large ears and sandy-grayish hair, and I knew that I was falling in love, and among other things I felt very foolish.

We said our names to each other: who would I be but Claire, the prodigal, as he later put it, and he of course was the Harvard-Boston shrink, the local prize and curiosity. Dr. C. S. Jones—Caleb Saltonstall—"My mother had some pretty embarrassing ambitions"—this too came later. Caleb.

Caleb and Claire.

We stood there laughing, like much younger, lighter-hearted people than we were.

I asked, "Do you want some iced tea, or something?" Why don't you touch me? We had not shaken hands.

He looked at his watch, and frowned unhappily. "I guess not, I've got a patient in twenty minutes." He looked at me.

And I, that formerly frightened, beaten down into self-hatred and ugliness—that young woman said, "Will you come back tonight? They all fall asleep about ten."

"Yes." We looked at each other again, but that quickly became too intense, my naked blue eyes into his dark brown, and we began to laugh—softly, this time, since we had just mentioned sleeping people. We wished that both now and tonight their sleep would be profound.

Hurriedly, I suppose to get things straight right away, I said, "I'm here with my son Simon. He's four. My husband's in San Francisco. Sort of a trial separation." I had not thought in those terms before, but those words, when said to Caleb, became true.

He hesitated for one instant. "Me too. Wife and kids in Boston. I keep so busy down here partly not to be besieged. God forbid I should be lonely. And I guess you'd call three thousand miles a separation, if not a trial."

We laughed, as all summer we were to laugh, at both the gravest and the most inconsequential matters. We laughed between our wildest encounters of love, and we talked almost not at all—and that, for that summer, for both of us was perfect.

He got up and we walked, touching shoulders in the accidental way that children might, toward his car. I said again, "You'll come around ten?"

"Of course."

By then he was sitting in his car, and I reached in, uncontrollably to touch his cheek.

Thus it was I who first invited, initiated, insisted— who first touched. And how lovely, with us, was the unimportance of that.

I went back into the house, where everyone was still asleep, where no one knew that anything important had occurred. Restless, elated and agitated, I walked through all those too-well-known overburdened rooms, staring at all the strange-familiar mahogany and silver, at heavy portraits of relatives who suddenly had a comical look of madness. At crazed mirrors which I considered crashing to the floor, so strong was my need for a commemorative gesture. At last in my wandering I came to the breakfast room (a room in which no one had ever had breakfast) where the phone was, and so, as though this had been my plan, I dialed my lover's San Francisco office, in itself a forbidden act. Collect.

Just after two, back there in San Francisco. He would quite possibly be just returned from lunch, possibly a little drunk.

He was, returned and drunk.

I said that I planned not to see him again, that it was all over. He said that he saw no reason whatsoever (a favorite lawyer word of his) for such a statement, nor for my call. I could imagine him sitting there, angrily twisting his too long legs—a way he has when exasperated. For good measure he threw in a few obscenities; I threw a few back, and hung up, feeling much better. Perhaps he did too? I would prefer to think not. But I had taken a step, my first for quite a while.

I took a long bath and put on a new light dress.

❧§❧

A little before six my father came downstairs, stretching and yawning and saying offhandedly, as though it were something I had already been told (this is an old trick of his), that Dudley Farmer and his wife and Mary Sue (my "old friend," the former belle who had inexplicably not yet married) were all coming by for drinks. In half an hour. I was thinking that in four more hours it would be ten, and Caleb would come; and so the impact of this information was less momentous than it might have been. I was not even frightened.

Dudley and his wife came first. She was a girl from another state, whom I had not met before, and for whom I felt an instant sympathy, a liking; it later occurred to me that we were somewhat alike.

But poor Dudley: my dangerous and violently handsome early love was muffled in fat, those terrific dark-blue eyes looked out, frightened, from folds of pale flesh. It was terrible: I wanted to hold him in my arms, to say, Don't worry, your operation won't be nearly as bad as you think it will be. Instead I embraced Simon, who had come in just then, so tardily awakened from his nap, and I introduced my son to my old friend.

They too liked each other on sight. My diffident difficult son told Dudley that he had never seen a cigarette lighter like the one Dudley had, and Dudley showed Simon how to use it, and how to light cigarettes for ladies, which Simon continued to do for the rest of that much too long cocktail hour.

(Three and a half more hours.)

Mary Sue arrived, and my first thought was: Well, she's got much better-looking, and at the same time I wondered if my brand-new feeling for Caleb would make me finally a kindly, charitable person. We greeted each other with that odd mixture of warmth and tentativeness which is seemingly the way of not quite old friends, and that odd brushing of cheeks that women do to each other, and I decided that yes, she did look better: thinner, a little sadder and certainly wiser than in her young and mindless, very popular days.

A thing to be said about Southern belles is that in fact

they are often not very pretty. Mary Sue at an early age was plump and nearsighted, with mouse-colored hair. However, she laughed easily and often, she was friendly and nonassertive and she kept that mousy hair in perfect curls, her nails a perfect pink. My mother, seeing me moping around the house on Saturday nights, in the months after Dudley's defection, used to say, "I do not see what those boys see in that Mary Sue. Tacky! Dumb! You wait, when that girl is thirty she's going to weigh two hundred pounds. Claire, you are one hundred times prettier than that girl." Just not saying, So how come you're sitting at home and she's out with the best-looking boy in town? How come Dudley dumped you for her? But my mother is often wrong: I was never all that much prettier than Mary Sue, and at thirty, a few years hence, thin Mary Sue was to marry an extremely successful architect, from Atlanta.

We all sat around on that porch where I had seemingly spent half my life just sitting around, and we talked in the desultory way that I was used to. No one asked any but the most perfunctory questions about my life in San Francisco; I need not have worried. Actually they probably did not believe that such a place existed.

However, there were some things I wanted to know, and I did ask, although circuitously. Had the schools changed much? Jobs for black people? Bussing? Well, I was told, there had been a little trouble here and there, but not bad at all, nothing like what had gone on in Beaumont and Hilton. Meaning: we here have better manners, we act better than people in other, even neighboring places.

"Has your mother taught you about collecting fire-flies in a fruit jar, to light up your room at night?" Dudley asked Simon. Of course I had not, and the three of us went into the kitchen to find some jars.

"You look really good," Dudley said to me. "Better than ever." His old grin.

"You look—" I began, not sure what I was going to say.

"I've got to get rid of fifteen more pounds before this lousy operation," he told me.

"When is it?"

"End of August."

"Well, worrying about operations is always the worst of them," I babbled. This may well be true, but I could not have known it was; I had only been hospitalized for the birth of Simon, to which I greatly looked forward. Having a child would win me favor with my husband, I then thought.

Back out on the porch everyone had more drinks, and Dudley, who was not drinking, took Simon down to the clumps of lilac at the edge of the lawn where the fireflies were, and he showed Simon how to capture them.

And at last everyone was gone, at last we had dinner and I put Simon to bed and my parents went upstairs to fall into their beds. And it was ten o'clock and I was out on the porch again, aware of veins that pulsed in my throat, and watching some fireflies that must have eluded Simon.

When I heard his car I wanted to run inside, upstairs and away from whatever was about to happen. Instead I sat there, as prim and proper (and as frightened) as I used to be when Dudley came to call. He—Caleb— came around the corner of the house and I got up and went down the stairs to meet him, and in a curious tense way we clasped each other, he a head taller than I—out there in the black sultry flower- and river-smelling night.

He said, "Let's go for a walk. I feel like walking."

That seemed a strange suggestion; I could have told

him of lovely private places to drive to, but he had already started out, nervous and fast, and so I followed.

And it seemed strange that he should be nervous. "I hadn't planned to fall in love with anyone," he later explained. "I never had—just with ideas. I knew you were dangerous," and he laughed.

At first I thought that he would want to talk, that this walk was for self-revelations, but it was not like that at all. We just walked, and every now and then he would ask a question, but always an immediate one. What kind of flower makes that very sweet smell? How old is that house? And further down the river, are there places to swim?

Once a pair of twin black cats came toward us out of the darkness, the country night—two cats thin and sleek and moving as one, long legs interwoven with each other, sometimes almost tripping. At that we laughed and stopped walking and laughed and laughed, both wondering (I suppose) if that was how we looked, although we were so upright.

Then we walked on, hurrying, like people with a destination, talking less, simply sensing each other, until seemingly we had made a circle, and we were back at my parents' house. Where, near the camellia bushes, for the first time we kissed. I thought that was a beginning, that our first night would last until sometime near morning, but Caleb meant to kiss me good night.

He won. Over all my clinging and whispered pleas that he stay, he said that he had an early patient. He had to go; he would come back the next day, and that night. And he was gone.

❧

He came back the next day just after lunch—I had told him about everyone's habits of naps.

It was a humid, hazy day. Everything looked heavier: the Spanish moss on the live oaks beside the river sagged lower toward the ground, wisteria vines hung heavily on their trellis.

He sat on the front steps, not having much time, my bare leg touching his bleached-out khaki pants. Caleb said, "I just can't believe this is happening to me. I'm a rational man—this is not my style at all."

I laughed, feeling amazingly light in the head and heart, unabashed, in the pounding sunshine. I said, "We have to go to a party this afternoon, but tonight? I'll see you tonight?"

❧

We all went to the party, my parents and Simon and I—and there, of course, among the old family friends, were Dudley and his wife. I talked mostly to her; disliking large parties, I "circulate" poorly, tend to stay with one person with whom I can talk. A dark pretty girl, with a soft voice from somewhere further south. I recognized that the quality I had felt in common with her was fear, but whereas I had been nebulously frightened of looming, dangerous people (who had already become somewhat unreal), she was worried about Dudley, simply and specifically. She said, "I really hope you'll come over and see us while you're here. Bring Simon, of course. But, until August—" And I said that she mustn't fuss or worry, feeling as kindly toward her as though she were an oldest friend. In fact I could see the emergence in myself of a calmer, kinder person, and I could feel that person reflected in the eyes of the old people who had known me all my life: they were thinking, Why, for heaven's sake, she's *nice*.

My father was talking about the Vietnam War, which was still going on at that time. "Well, I'm neither a hawk nor a dove, but a *bustard*," he said, as he was to say often over the summer (and I to cringe: my calm kindness had its limits). "Has anyone ever heard of that fabulous old bird? A native of Pakistan, I do believe."

➥&#65533;➤

That night in his beat-up car Caleb and I drove down the narrow tarred road, down along the river to a small clearing in the tropical tangle of Spanish moss and honeysuckle vines. We got out and in the heavy blackness we found the narrow beach, of coarse river sand, and there, at last, we made love. God knows what we said—I think not much at all.

That day, and that night began the pattern of my summer: days of walks and swims with Simon, frequent parties with my parents, old friends. Some encounters with Dudley and his wife, less frequently with Mary Sue. Nights with Caleb, plus a few infrequent daylight intervals; he was allowing himself to be overworked at the hospital, for reasons of his own. Also he was worried about his helpless charges. And working on a book.

I don't think that Caleb and I needed the excitement of illicitness; we simply wanted privacy, which was not easy in that town. But, "For secret lovers, we spend a lot of time outdoors, don't we?" Caleb remarked one night, as we lay on our tiny private beach in the dark. "I'm sure it's terribly healthy for us," he said, and we laughed like idiots.

Making love, laughing. That is what we did, that summer, both to excess; in both cases, having once started, we seemed unable to stop. Little talk, no plans—it was *marvelous*. I thought about Caleb all day; he was always in my mind, but with no anxiety, which I found amazing. Love and fear had always arrived together, for me, before.

170

I often forgot what Caleb did, his profession—or, rather, I didn't think about it. But he said a few things from such extraordinary insight that I thought, What an amazingly good doctor he must be. One thing that he said was "I think you're going to take a while getting used to being happy." That was true; it has taken years.

⟐

Sometimes—being already naked, Caleb and I—we slipped into the river and swam about in the warm black almost unmoving water. Remembered, this seems a dangerous thing to have done, for obvious reasons; at the time it seemed natural and easy—the river was there for us, as we were for each other.

⟐

Simon, too, thrived during that summer. He got taller, his hair lighter and his skin dark brown; and no one told him to be quiet or to finish his hamburger. With neighboring children he waded in the river and played with boats, his unaccented California voice mingling with their slower, softer speech.

⟐

I wrote to my husband and said that since this was, in fact, a separation, and it seemed to be working out (I cited Simon, his height and his happiness), perhaps we should consider a divorce. I had no clear plans involving Caleb, whose own life was obscure to me (it was one of the things we did not talk about), and I knew that in any case I would have to go back to San Francisco in the fall to straighten things out, as Caleb would have to go back to Boston. I wrote about a divorce simply to have it stated, to have something begun. My most definite plan was to move from that flat, with the live-in downstairs landlady. I would find a place with a wooded open setting, in a quiet neighborhood, perhaps on Twin Peaks or Potrero Hill, where Simon and I would feel at home. That seemed most important.

☙≈❧

"We don't talk much, do we?" Caleb one night remarked, as, uncharacteristically, we sat in a booth in the New Athens, braving public opinion. Drinking beer. "Considering how much I think about us," he added.

"Do we have to? I love our not talking," I truthfully told him.

"I guess not." And then he said, "You know, sometimes you're so beautiful it hurts."

☙≈❧

My husband responded rather tersely that he would talk to me when I got back to San Francisco; like so many lawyers, he hates to commit himself to the written word.

Looking back, I suppose it is surprising that I did not mention this exchange to Caleb; at the time it did not occur to me to do so.

☙≈❧

And then without warning the summer began to rush toward fall. Even in that warm Southern air there was a hint of cooler days to come. It was almost the end of August, time for me to make reservations to go back (not "home") to San Francisco.

It was time for Dudley Farmer's operation.

The operation went well; Caleb called me from the hospital to tell me that. The surgeon was pleased. Of course Dudley would be in Intensive Care for a couple of days, but then I could go to see him.

I called the airline office and made our reservations. Twelve more days, which at the time seemed both infinite, a treasure, and like no time at all, like nothing.

Ten more days.

Because it is very late at night, Caleb and I are going for a walk instead of driving down to our beach. There is a light warm breeze that ruffles the dried-out, end-of-summer grasses at the edge of the road. And suddenly through the grasses come those two black cats—they are somewhat larger but they must be the same ones; surely no other two cats have this impossible way of walking, their legs weaving together.

Caleb and I stop walking and we begin to laugh, laughing softly, chokingly, in the black stirring night, until we are weak and we sit down in the field beside the road, and after a while, because it is so dark and we are lying there, we make love where we are.

Seven more days, a week. Over her third lunchtime sherry my mother has said that I may pick all the flowers I can find in the wilting garden, and I do just that; I make an enormous bouquet of overblown roses and crape myrtle and gardenias and camellias and I surround it all with magnolia leaves, and I take it to the hospital, to Dudley.

Walking through those greenish corridors, through swinging steel doors and forbidding alien smells, I am irrationally frightened, and I feel a lurch of sympathy for poor Dudley, incarcerated here, at the mercy of those brisk and stiffly uniformed people.

At the desk, on his floor, I am told that he cannot have visitors, not that day. My flowers are taken, will be given to him. I do not see his wife.

❧

Six more days. Something has gone wrong, Caleb tells me. Dudley is bleeding internally. A hemorrhage.

❧

Simon would like to write to all his new friends from San Francisco. He would like to send them cards of the Golden Gate Bridge, the cable cars, things like that. Will I help him? Could he learn to write? I say yes to both questions, and I note to myself that he is making more detailed plans for the winter than I am.

❧

Dudley died two days before I was to fly West. Caleb came early in the afternoon to tell me that. Everyone was asleep and I was sitting on the steps, and it could have been the start of summer, except that it was not.

"It was one of those inexplicable medical horrors," Caleb said. "Why doctors feel basically helpless, or they should. A sudden infection, from nowhere."

I had begun to cry, for too many reasons. Caleb put his arms around me; if anyone passed and saw us we no longer cared. (I have since learned that everyone in town knew all—or almost all—about us anyway, of course.)

To me almost the worst of it was that Dudley had had to spend his last months so fat and frightened, dreading what he must darkly have known would happen.

❧

Caleb had a staff meeting that night, and I had a dinner party. Impossible to meet, although I had a dim sense that earlier in our heady, impetuous summer we would have worked it out.

"Reality has hit us," Caleb said, unhappily. "Christ, why can't we run backwards to June?"

In a brief exhausted way we talked about what to do the following night, our last; we even considered my saying, "I'm going out to dinner with Caleb Jones." But the prospect of saying those words was jarring; we would have felt invaded. And then there was the problem of Simon, whom (significantly) Caleb had never met.

We decided to do what we always did, to meet at ten.

❧

And so the next night I had dinner with my parents, who got a little drunker than usual, I suppose out of a feeling that this was a festive occasion, and with Simon, who (I thought) was curiously callous about the end of his good summer, among new friends. He was excited about San Francisco.

❧

That night Caleb and I talked far too much, and I especially said all the wild and impossible things that all summer I had managed not to say: I said that I had

175

never loved anyone else, I never would, et cetera. Caleb responded reasonably enough that I was too young to predict my future feelings, that he could not accept such promises. Besides, he said, he was almost totally involved in his work, to an extent that I had not understood; also, he was basically not a terribly emotional person. Personal relationships were not, or had not been, of prime importance to him.

I wept, feeling abandoned and feeling too that I had managed to wreck the whole summer. In any case, that was our worst, our only bad time together. So that by the time we stopped talking and made love we were half asleep.

❧❦❧

Back in San Francisco, not hearing from Caleb (I wrote him all the time, somewhat hysterically, trying to re-create our summer) and missing him, at first I was depressed; I felt almost as beaten down and helpless as before I had left.

But the weather that fall was cool and clear and lovely, and I seemed, somehow, to have acquired over the summer a more positive view, and some strength: I told my husband that I wanted a divorce, that I was going to find a new place to live, and a job.

And then, like a reward, a letter came from Caleb. Not at all a crazy impassioned one, as mine had been, but one that was rational and friendly, kind. He said that he had been too depressed to write before, and that sometimes, even, our summer seemed unreal to him. But I felt wonderful; reading his letter restored me. And, interestingly, the next day I found an apartment on a quiet wooded street, on the western slope of Twin Peaks.

My divorce, also, went astoundingly well; my husband made none of the trouble that I would have expected of him. (It later turned out that he wanted to marry his secretary—such an original man!)

Simon and I moved into our good new place; he went to a new school and I got a part-time job in a doctor's office. And I began to "go out," to have a good time.

Caleb and I continued to write to each other, I much more frequently than he, but that was all right; I assumed that he was busier, and in a curious way I did not expect certain things from Caleb. He did not say that he was living with his wife and children, but I assumed that to be the case. Why not? is how he would think of it.

Even when I eventually fell in love with someone else I continued to write to Caleb, not telling him about the other man (although somehow I felt that he would know, and not mind).

One night—I think in February: a cold swirling fog-bound night—during a lonely rift with the other man, I again wrote to Caleb, somewhat in my old tone. In part, I said to him, "I think you saved my life last summer, I will really always love you."

And, the next morning, which was a cleared spring-suggesting day, I reread that letter and was surprisingly unembarrassed by it. I sent it off.

❧

Caleb's book was successful. He became famous.

❧

And later I married the other man, and later still I almost got used to being happy.

177

A Pale and Perfectly
Oval Moon

Dying, for a time Penelope Moore behaved atrociously. To her husband, Van, who loved her (in his way), both the fact of her dying and her continuous, ferociously whispered accusations were intolerable.

She was supposed to have died early in the summer. "To be quite honest, old man, I'm surprised she lasted through the spring," the friendly internist whose charge she was had said to Van in June. But June had passed, July, August, September; and in the middle of October still she "lingered on," as the false old phrase would have it. As Penelope herself cried out, "My God, I'm lingering on—is that what *ma*lingering comes from, do you suppose? Have you thought of that? God, why am I still *here?*"

"Here," practically speaking, was the Moores' country weekend house, on a bend in a river, in California's High Sierras. It was a house that a local contractor had thrown together, somewhat hastily, on speculation— and which the Moores had bought on a hasty impulse. It was not well planned: some rooms, the master bedroom and the kitchen, were impractically large and drafty; the dining-living room was small and cramped. But outside the shingles had weathered beautifully, turning silver in the strong clear air, at that altitude, and Penelope had always loved the house's many-windowed openness, its proximity to the outdoors, and to the seasons. A New Englander, Penelope had remarked often before they bought this house that she literally could not bear the California lack of seasons. Windows gave either onto the meadow or the river, so that the house was full of rushing river sounds.

And now that she was so sick the too large bedroom did not seem an inconvenience: the table that held her drugs and other terrible accoutrements of her illness could be screened off, and a cot for Van had been placed beside the large old double bed, and on the other side a big comfortable chair. Although, should she "linger" through the winter, Van wondered how he could keep the house warm enough, could defend it against windows packed with snow. A neighbor, Miss Bird, a former nurse, had moved into the guest room to help with the care of Penelope. The local hospital was excellent, and near. (Everything might have been planned.)

Van was a lawyer with a small office in San Francisco—two partners, one harassed secretary. Therefore it was necessary for him to return to the city at intervals to keep things going, or to try to. Sometimes he drove the three hours there and back in a day; at other, less frequent times he stayed overnight in their Twin Peaks flat.

"Of course you have to spend the night," Penelope hissed on these occasions. "You have to get laid, and who would expect a man of your age to arise from some floozy's bed and drive for hours up into the mountains with a sick and thankless wife at the end of the trip?"

"Now, Pen, come on—"

Always pale, her pallor now had a cast that was almost blue—like moonlight on snow, Van uncharacteristically thought, but was unhappily not able to say, although he dimly knew that it was a thing she would like to have heard.

He also liked the floating pale scarves she wore, to hide the terribly thinning patchy hair, and he did not say that either.

"Tell me, will you tell me something I want to know?" asked Penelope furiously. "Do you really like those southern Italian girls, or Mexicans best? Oh, I know, as long as they're dark and sort of sleazy you don't much care. The most beautiful girl I ever knew was Corsican—thick, thick black hair and wild eyes and the sexiest mouth. My God, why couldn't you have met Maria? Why me? It's like the end of Proust, where Swan says that he's ruined his life for a woman who was not his type at all."

"I fell in love with you," said Van, quite truthfully.

"In love. Jesus. Well, have a divine time in the city. With whoever." She sighed, and in an instant had fallen into one of her short but deep and blessed sleeps.

Van went into the kitchen and told Miss Bird that he was going.

Outside Penelope's windows, the October landscape showed an extraordinary spectrum of yellow: the wild-rose bush that grew beside the door was pinkish yellow, next to the brighter-yellow lilac leaves. Out in the meadow the grasses were yellow green, and the yellow yarrow bloomed there still. Beside the river, willow leaves had turned to rust; in the dark rapids ridiculous birds, called bobbers, dipped and swam, and across the water, from a stand of aspens, fluttered the most brilliant yellow of all, as clear and pure as sunlight.

❦

Van's floozy—he both winced and was amused at Penelope's word—was in fact a pleasant and quite

180

unspectacular girl named Joan, who had arrived in the office as a Kelly Girl, to help out the overburdened secretary. Neither Italian nor Mexican, in fact Scottish, Joan had pale-brown hair, more or less the color that Penelope's had been.

"What you don't understand," Van sometimes imagined saying to Penelope, as he drove the seemingly endless three-hour trip away from her, toward San Francisco and Joan, "what you don't understand is that I might stare at those big sexy dark girls, or I might make a pass at one of them at a party, if I'd had enough to drink. But ten years ago it was you, you with what you continue to call your dirty-blond hair, that I fell in love with. And now for quite another kind of love there is Joan." Impossible, of course, to say this to Penelope, and he found it harder and harder to talk to her at all. What can you say to someone who knows that she is dying, and who continuously rages at that deprivation?

❦

In fact, Van had had one and only one affair with the sort of girl who Penelope insisted was his "type." She had been a woman of dazzling darkness, of a vast and careless voluptuousness. He had loved her wildly for a time, and the repeated failures of their acts of love had been to him a bitter and amazing disappointment. This was shortly before he met Penelope, who unfortunately remembered seeing him with his "dark prize" (her phrase) at a party some months earlier.

He had fallen in love at once with Penelope; she had been an enchantment to him, stirring all his senses—a wild delight.

She was at that time a thin young woman, divorced, with no children; she lived scantily on a part-time job in an art gallery. Her two manias, both unfamiliar to Van, were for chamber music and for conversation. When

181

she wasn't listening to music—composers he hadn't heard of before: Telemann, Hummel, Boccherini—she was passionately talking, examining, commenting, then laughing a lot at it all. She read a lot of novels. They married rather hastily, they were often happy and sometimes they quarreled. And then she was sick— then dying.

❧

Aside from the color of her hair, Joan, Van's Kelly Girl, his "floozy," was as unlike Penelope as one woman could be to another. Soft and plump, Joan was so passive, so vague and dreamy in manner that at first, hiring her, Van had nervously wondered if she was stupid—or possibly drugged. But as she sat at her typewriter, looking tranced, her fingers literally flew over the keys, and her work was perfect: the most abstruse words correctly spelled, the legal forms all exact, and all this was produced with a speed that was embarrassing to the other, regular secretary. Joan was not dumb. Eventually Van decided that she was concentrated on some unknown area of her own mind, which he was never to discover.

❧

The "affair"—Van did not quite think of it as that; in fact he had no words for what went on between them, and tended to use Penelope's: "floozy," "getting laid," although he liked Joan, and meant no disrespect— whatever it was had begun predictably enough. On a certain evening last spring Van had an unavoidable dinner engagement with clients. Also, there was more immediately important work than Joan could finish by five—papers that Van had to take with him to court early the following morning. "No sweat," said Joan, in her pleasant passive way, lifting moony brown eyes to Van's darker brown. "I live sort of near you, on Ashbury, and I've got a machine like this at home. You could stop and pick up the stuff on your way by."

Somehow what came through to him as most odd in this statement was the fact that she had such an expensive piece of office machinery at home, an IBM Selectric, but being hard-pressed he accepted her offer without much thought.

The dinner with clients, at a "top" French restaurant, was carelessly seasoned and terribly expensive— was boring and unproductive. Driving away from it, having drunk an unnecessary final brandy, Van was assaulted by one of the awful and engulfing waves of self-pity that normally he was able to fight off. In that dark and rainy moment, driving through snarls of downtown night traffic, he saw himself as the hard-working husband of an ungratefully dying woman.

And it was more or less in that mood that he arrived at Joan's apartment, in the neighborhood that five years back had been loosely designated as "the Haight."

Concerned with himself, Van had not thought about Joan and her possible surroundings; probably he would have imagined plants and posters, what he thought of as the trappings of the young. Certainly he was not prepared for such visible luxury, so much soft pale leather, such a heavy bronze-bound glass coffee table, on which there was a huge jar of exotic flowers. In fact his look of surprise, on that first entrance, was enough to cause her to say, though softly, "I made a lot of money in the Sixties, when anyone could." (Weeks later, in a moment of intimacy, he could ask how—how had she got so rich, so young? "Dealing, mostly." And when at first he did not understand she said, "Just grass, and sometimes acid. Never anything hard, and I don't deal at all anymore." She liked the variety of life as a Kelly Girl.)

Nor was he prepared for the mild and friendly pleasures of being in bed with Joan, which he was, rather soon, that first night. "Love," or whatever it was with Joan, was so totally unlike what love had been with Penelope that his guilt was decreased (a little); with Joan there were no wild sensual flights, there was no amazement. Ease and warmth and friendliness were what he felt with Joan. Some gratitude. Some guilt.

The guilt in fact went in both directions—or, rather, toward both women. Guilt toward Joan because he spent so little time with her, never more than an hour, sometimes less; even when he was staying overnight in town he left her scrupulously early and went back to his own place to sleep, back to his own phone.

Guilt toward Penelope because he was unable to keep her from dying.

⤙§⤚

Now, in the bright and boring sunshine, the relentless three hours of the trip to San Francisco, Van was mildly thinking of Joan, whom he expected to see that night. He even (improbably) imagined a conversation about her with Penelope. "Not quite your ordinary Kelly Girl," he imagined himself saying—to Penelope, who had sometimes accused him of being square. "She made a lot of money during the Sixties selling dope. Sort of an interesting woman."

But, along with the too familiar smell of onions at Vacaville, an equally familiar depression settled into his mind. What, *really,* was so interesting about selling dope? Joan was not an interesting woman; Penelope was. Joan was simply very nice.

One of the things that Van most hated about this

184

drive, both ways, was his obsessive fear that Penelope might die while he was on the highway, locked into speeding steel and burning rubber, into the screaming monotony of a superhighway. She could die while he was concentrated on passing a giant diesel freight truck, straining on the final lap of its cross-country haul—could die while he was passing the tollbooth at Vallejo and thinking, Thirty more miles.

Arrived at his office, in a converted Victorian house out on Pine Street, Van was informed by his secretary that his anticipated business lunch had been canceled—good: more uncluttered time for work. Miss Gibson had called—Joan, currently a Kelly Girl at an office somewhere in the Jack Tar Building. A court date had been shifted forward into December. A client had called to complain about his bill.

Van calculated: if he worked through lunchtime, ordering something, he could spend that extra couple of hours taking Joan out to dinner—a thing that he had never done, and felt badly about not doing. He could still go to bed early in his own Twin Peaks place, and be up early and back to work as planned.

But Miss Joan Gibson was unavailable on the phone, out of the office on an errand, or something, and it was midafternoon before Van reached her, and rather proudly invited her out for dinner.

"Wow, that sounds so nice," she said. "But of all the lousy breaks—my father's in town today."

"Your father?" She had never mentioned a father, and for a single instant it occurred to Van that she might be lying. But Joan wouldn't lie; she didn't need to. She would have said, as she had a couple times before, "I'm really sorry, but I've got something else that I have to do."

And now she laughed, softly and pleasantly. "Yes, my father. He lives in Salt Lake; he's sort of a nice old guy. You'd like him. But I guess that's not such a neat idea."

"No, I guess not. Well, I hope I'll see you soon."

"Yes, really. And I'm sorry about tonight. Call me when you get back down, O.K.?"

Such was the friendly and casually intimate tone of their connection. Leaving the phone, Van was smiling to himself.

Then, recalculating his time and his work, he saw that if he again ordered something portable at his desk for dinner, and continued to work, he would be entirely through by nine or ten at the latest. He would not have to stay over; he could be back up in the mountains with Penelope by midnight or so.

He had a ham-and-cheese sandwich for dinner, and coffee, and he left the office at a little after nine.

And by eleven that night he had passed Auburn, and begun the third and final hour of his journey, the sixty miles or so of ascent into the mountains, from two to six thousand feet.

On either side of the highway, in the darkness, the black shapes of trees diminished as he climbed, and at last he was up in a barren and lonely landscape of rocks, of stretching waste.

Suddenly, near Donner Summit, the yellow edge of the rising moon appeared from behind an outcropping of rocks. A ridiculously shaped oval moon, a perfect egg—a Humpty-Dumpty moon that disappeared behind a rock as quickly, and as foolishly, as it had arisen.

Penelope was awake.

"Darling, what a lovely surprise," she said, in a voice from months or years ago. She was sitting up in bed, reading by lamplight, with something pale and floating about her head.

Van kissed her cheek, and then sat in the bedside chair. He told her about getting his work done, mentioning cases that he had talked about before. His trip home. The moon. "It was really a ludicrous moon. It looked just like Humpty-Dumpty," he said.

And Penelope laughed—her old light laugh that had once seemed to touch his skin like lace.

❧

Remission. That was the word that Miss Bird whispered to Van as they both witnessed Penelope during the next few days, then weeks. But Van rejected the word; he knew that he was in the presence of a miracle.

Outside, in the bright cool October air, the leaves slowly darkened from yellow to burnished gold, and in the house the rooms were full of the sounds of flutes and clarinets, of violins and cellos—Brahms and Schubert, Boccherini, Telemann.

Which is not to say that Penelope was really *well:* when, as she infrequently did, she got out of bed and moved around the house, her movements were painfully, haltingly slow. But she talked a lot now—gently, amusingly, affectionately. She was so nearly her old self that it was hard for Van not to hope: perhaps she could be like this for years?

Only once—on the day, in fact, of the first snowfall of that season, a light white dusting that lay softly among the meadow grass—on that day, with the most terrible sadness, Penelope asked, "Do you know what this is like?" (She did not have to explain what she meant by "this.") "It's like having to separate from someone you're wildly in love with. When you desperately think that you'd give twenty years of your life for another hour together. I wonder if maybe that's what

I've done. Taken extra hours. Made that bargain, somehow. Sometime."

Unbearably moved, at the same time Van experienced a spurt of jealousy. About whom had she felt such a desperate love? Not for him; their love affair had been passionate but without despair. No anguished separations. He himself had felt such desperation for his "dark prize," a feeling that he had forgotten, or that did not occur to him now.

But then smilingly Penelope said, "Van, darling, I do feel guilty about your staying up here so much, but of course it is lovely," and she reached to touch his hand with her white, white blue-veined hand.

She even looked, in a way, quite wonderful: the vague pale scarves about her head intensified the darkness of her eyes, the firm small structure of her nose. You look beautiful, he wanted to say, but he was afraid of a sound of mockery.

❧

Early in the summer after Penelope died, Van married Joan. (Penelope died, as he had feared, while he was on the road, during one of those horrendously dull blurs between Auburn and San Francisco, early in November.) Van and Joan moved her expensive possessions up the hill from her Ashbury apartment to his Twin Peaks flat.

It all worked out quite well, including the furniture, which fit. Joan stopped being a Kelly Girl and took cooking lessons, and became a skillful cook. They made love often, and for the most part happily.

The only problem was—that Van was just slightly bored. As he had surmised some time ago, Joan was not a very interesting woman. But he didn't really mind this touch of boredom; it left him more time to himself. Since they talked rather little, Van began to read books that he had "always meant" to read. Novels, in fact, that Penelope had recommended. Proust, *Middlemarch*, *Anna Karenina* and, finally, *Wuthering Heights*, which made him weep—all alone, over a final brandy.

In fact, since Joan was a person who lived most vitally during the day (her favorite time for love was on waking, in the morning), and who often went to bed very early, Van took to drinking a little too much late at night, alone, confronted with his dark and sprawling city view of the lightscattered San Francisco hills. Penelope had been a night person; she had chosen this flat for its spectacular night view.

He had sold the mountain house soon after Penelope died, at a loss, because he was unable to imagine a stay up there without her. And now sometimes he dreamily imagined that he was back in the mountains, imagined that the actual sounds of traffic below his windows were river sounds, and that he was with Penelope.

Unhappily it was not always a loving and gentle Penelope that he believed he was with; he could remember Penelope the shrew quite accurately. (Had she been shrewish on purpose so that he would miss her less? He could believe that of complex Penelope.)

But now when she hissed that he didn't love her, that she was not his type—now he could say, and strongly enough to convince her, "You're the most remarkable and interesting woman I've ever known. I've never really loved anyone but you."

Attrition

The Xs are moving to Israel, and I am taking it badly; I am in near-mourning over their imminent loss. If it were another couple—non-friends, or non-close friends—I would probably think, Oh, how nice, a new start, how adventurous. Or, if I were a nicer, more imaginative and generous person (possibly sometimes I am, but not this month, this winter), I might think, Oh, how great for Judith and Daniel X.

orn

This is January, in San Francisco, and we are having a heat wave. For a while it was fun, walking around Pacific Heights in jeans and a cotton shirt, among the deceived and unnaturally flowering blossom trees, in the middle of winter. A woman up the street, sitting on her front steps with her bare legs outstretched to the sun, remarked to me, "Well, this year we don't have to go to Palm Springs."

But then it became ominous, such heat and dryness, with no snow falling up in the Sierras. There are headlines about drought, water shortages, dying cattle, meat prices—and no sign of rain.

A few weeks ago I went to a large rather elaborate dinner party: mostly older people, mostly rich. And when it came time to go home I could not find the small black silk bag I had brought. The composition of the party made theft fairly unlikely; still, there is always the closet kleptomaniac. There was nothing in the purse except a compact and lipstick and comb, and the bag itself had not been expensive, but it was pretty, the simple sort of envelope that is inexplicably hard to find.

I am not sure why I bring this up. I suppose to add, by way of contrast, a minor loss.

What I am saying is: I think I am reacting in an extreme way to the departure of the Xs partly because the world seems to me to be getting worse.

I do not even have the excuse of their being oldest, long-term friends. (My oldest friend, in fact another Judith, lives in Washington, D.C.; she is a terrible correspondent.) I have only known the Xs for a couple of years. But I like them both enormously; perhaps it would be more accurate to say that I love them.

Judith and Daniel. Both dark, very attractive, strong and healthy and intelligent people. Married for a long time, four children who are grown and gone. They still like each other. To put it negatively, they are not crazy or destructive people. Daniel smokes too much but that is the worst thing I can say about either of them.

My son just called to say that his grandfather had died, the father of my first husband, from whom I am divorced. The old man was once powerfully wicked, monstrously *present* in my life, but I no longer think of him. Simon, my son, and I agree that many people, including his father, will be relieved, and rich. Still.

I tell Simon that the Xs are moving to Israel; he has met and liked them.

He says, "If I were moving anywhere I'd rather live in Wales."

Wales? As far as I know, none of our people are from there. England, Scotland, Ireland. But is that important?

Will Simon inherit enough money to move to Wales?

❧⸏❧

Daniel X inherited a business that he did not much like, but, having married very young and been so young a father, he was rather stuck with it. He was a good sport, not complaining, but anyone could see that he was better suited to a more intellectual calling; he could have been a physicist, a mathematician, perhaps a poet. And now in early middle age he is to be free of that business, to sell it and emigrate. (One of the X daughters has said, "Other parents get divorced, or die. You *emigrate*.") While her youngest child was in high school Judith studied social work; now she works in a clinic in my neighborhood. I walk a lot, and sometimes I drop in, and if she is free we talk for five or ten minutes. Often she is busy, but she always manages to convey warmth and welcome anyway; this is one of her special skills.

Do I begin to convey what I will miss?

Voracious novel reading is a common ground. Last year Daniel insisted that I read *Something Happened,* which I had lazily put off; so *long.* And he was right, it is wonderful. And we recommend good rereads to each other. Judith recently rediscovered *Middlemarch,* Daniel reread *Moby Dick* and *The Possessed.* (In general, he is fond of Russian novels, whereas Judith and I are more apt to read the English.) I reread *Great Expectations* and some Trollope.

(My private formula for a depression is all of Jane Austen; it may be time for her now.)

Everyone, or everyone I know, feels warmly and strongly about the Xs. Only once did I hear a negative remark about them, and that was from a harsh, competitive woman, Ms. Z, who was, I believe, simply tired of hearing Judith, in particular, so much praised. "Well," said Ms. Z. (She has an especially unpleasant voice: loud and condescending, with a fake "Eastern" accent.) "Well, I really feel that most of her relationships are very superficial." Though hostile, Ms. Z is not stupid; there may have been a sort of truth in her remark, if she meant that Judith's friends are less important to her than she to them. (Another truth may be that Judith's feelings for Ms. Z are superficial.) I for one don't mind. I accept the fact that her husband and children are the center of Judith's life—and Israel; she has always had a strong emotional-ideological attachment to Israel. Both she and Daniel come from originally Central European Jewish families who suffered horrors under Hitler—agonizing deaths and deprivations; of course they feel strongly about Israel.

They have often visited there. They love it.

Israel. I see deserts and sand dunes, modern architecture superimposed on ancient cities. Scholars and statesmen. Chaim Weizmann, Golda Meir. Maps, arrows, darkened areas of trouble. Televised wars.

❧⚶❧

In a way I envy this attachment of the Xs to another country. When, as increasingly happens, I cannot stand the directions taken by this one—the support of wars and governments that I hate, the nonsupport of the old and sick and poor—I am sadly aware of having nowhere else to go. I love northern Italy, and southern France, but I don't think I could live in either place.

I would think that you have to be passionately committed to Israel to live there. Possibly you have to be Jewish?

So, then, a part of my reaction is envy? I might have known.

❧⚶❧

At the same party at which I lost my black silk bag, an old, ill-looking man was talking a lot about how terrible Cesar Chavez is, mentioning wetbacks, Kennedys, Catholics and more wetbacks. I said at last that although not a wetback, a Kennedy nor even a Catholic, I admired Mr. Chavez very much.

He thought I was accusing him of calling me a wetback. Hopeless confusion. He sputtered off, enraged, his face a darker, more unhealthy mottled red.

I wonder: is it possible that he stole my bag, hoping to find subversive literature, or dope? Or could he be the closet kleptomaniac (or *queen*)? I would love for these things to be true, any of them, but I am afraid he is simply a sick reactionary.

❦

As I have not said so far, I too am part of a couple. And I suppose our relationship with the Xs is characteristic of such couple friendships: the strong bond is between Judith and me. The men like each other well enough but without us, the women, they would probably not know each other.

Daniel is an extremely attractive man, but (fortunately) I am never turned on by husbands of women I like. I would guess that Judith is the same.

❦

Judith calls, and because we so infrequently speak on the phone at first I don't recognize her voice. But then I do, and I begin to make concealing jokes about how terrible it is that they are leaving.

She laughs in her affectionate way, and she says, "Oh, you're really wonderful—I love you—yours is really the best reaction. Everyone else is saying how great."

I tell her that I am just entirely selfish.

"Well, what are you doing now?"

"Now?"

"Why don't you two come over for dinner? I'm making some veal."

(Judith is an exceptional cook. Of course.)

❦

My husband (my third: Israel is not all that I envy Judith for; this one is nice, usually, but the two divorces were not nice at all), this husband says, comfortingly, "Well, maybe they're not really serious. You know, it could be just an idea."

I laugh gratefully. "Like the way I talk about moving to Verona?"

"Yes, sort of like that."

☙

In this crazy weather I never know what to wear; it's even hot at night. I settle on a favorite long summer cotton dress.

☙

As we walk toward their house we can see Judith and Daniel through their front windows; and somehow, sinkingly, from their postures I know that they are serious about Israel.

"Serious" is in fact the correct word to describe that evening. Despite good wines and superlative (as always) food, none of us is light-hearted.

We have come there, really, to hear in detail the Xs' plans, and we do; we hear all about it, we argue and concede.

They are going to sell everything, Daniel says: his business, their comfortable large house—this house— and their summer country cabin. My husband, in many ways a practical man (although a sculptor, an excellent one, and he teaches at a local art school)—he suggests that they rent this house for a while, instead of selling, and have the rent as income, there in Israel.

"No." Daniel has thought of and rejected this. "I want to go there completely committed. We're not just sticking our toes in the water."

They will go, then, with a fair amount of money. Which they are going to use to buy or invest in a new business: an English language bookstore. They are informed that there is room for such a shop in Jerusalem, which is where they want to live. The book business appeals strongly to them both, and we have to admit that it makes sense.

(Now, this is curious: the more definite their intentions sound, the better I am able to accept them. As one would a clear diagnosis—I am not glad, not at all, but merely sad, rather than darkly depressed.)

By the end of the evening we are saying that we will all meet glamorously in Rome, or that we will come to visit them in Jerusalem.

"You'd really love it." Judith is sure.

We go home more or less cheered.

❦

But sometime after midnight, at some terrible pre-dawn hour, suspended between black and gray light, I begin to think of the four people whom I knew well who have died this year. Cancer (two), emphysema, a suicide. It has seemed a year of death, of thinking of death, living near it. And then I see that in my list I forgot Simon's grandfather, who died of a heart ailment. Five.

I believe that several epidemics are going on.

❦

That morning, getting up, we see that one of those violently wrenched changes in the weather has occurred, to which we in San Francisco seem fated. (It is surprising that we don't all have pneumonia, often.) It is extremely cold; the sky is black, with menacing clouds, and a harsh wind blows, and blows. Surely now it will rain?

But it doesn't rain. By noon the clouds have disappeared, and the day is brilliant with sunshine, although still very cold. And then, in late afternoon, the clouds come back. But still no rain.

❧§❧

Actually, my husband and I have not been getting along especially well. Nothing terrible, and nothing definite; simply—a slackening of whatever tensions have drawn and held us together. A lessening of warmth, of interest. We talk less. We spend more hours at home in separate rooms.

My first two husbands were both doctors. Perhaps a sculptor is too radical a change?

Are there any solutions?

❧§❧

My son telephones. His grandfather's will has been read, and he will "come into," as the phrase goes, quite a lot of money.

(Will he go to Wales?)

"Simon, that's terrific," I say, concealing fear (I think). "Whatever will you do with all that?"

I am notoriously stupid about money; ludicrous for me to advise him; besides he is too old.

"I think I'll buy a pair of flats on Potrero Hill." Potrero, across the city from Pacific Heights, is a looser, more varied neighborhood than this upper-middle-class one, where Simon grew up. "With that much of a down payment I could pay it all off soon with rents, and have some income left."

Simon is a painter (he and this husband get along very well); this seems a wonderfully practical solution for him. I am amazed, really delighted.

"A building on top of one of the hills. I could have the top floor for a studio," he is saying.

Sometimes Simon makes me think that there is, after all, some hope for the rest of us.

❦

That night, half asleep, I hear a curious small steady sound, which I do not understand. But it is not the rain, which by now we do desperately need.

The next morning, still sleepy, I get up first and walk toward the front of the house, and gradually I become aware that outside, beyond the windows, something extraordinary is happening. *Snow!* I call out, "Snow!" waking my husband, alarming the cats. "Look—snow!"

It never snows in San Francisco (the last real snowfall was in 1876) but there it is: white on the rooftops of cars parked along the street, and still coming down— softly, gently, with infinite delicacy. A miracle.

❦

Bundled in sheepskin, wearing boots, I go out for a walk. Light snow feathers my face—it is lovely!

I head for the clinic where Judith works, and there she is, also in sheepskin but hers is white; she bought it in Israel. She is coming out the door as I approach. She says happily, "A patient just canceled and I thought I'd walk down to the park. See the trees with snow."

"Marvelous."

People are driving more slowly than usual; everyone looks about with a sort of wonderment.

We reach the Presidio, the woods: eucalyptus, bent cypresses and pines, today are all dusted over with white, although it is no longer snowing. It is *very* beautiful, as Judith and I say to each other.

Then Judith says, "When friends from Israel come to see us, we always bring them here, and sometimes out

199

to Muir Woods. You know, they have so few trees there."

This remark, rather sadly spoken, remains in my mind, with echoes. And for the first time it occurs to me that we are not, after all, entirely opposed on this issue of their going to Israel. It is not as though Judith had no misgivings about their move, and I no good wishes for them.

I say, "But you'll come back sometimes to visit?"

"Oh, of course. We've got our parents, and all the kids, and *you*."

We laugh at this, but I do feel better.

⋙❧⋘

That afternoon it occurs to me that perhaps some ceremony or ritual would help, and I choose the one available to my age and social group: a party. We will give a party for the Xs, a farewell party. It is strange that I had not thought of this before: my husband and I like to give parties; it is something that we do well together. We have worked out a formula that is somewhere between a cocktail party and a buffet dinner (we both dislike both those labels). It is just a party, with a lot of food and drink.

⋙❧⋘

Judith is delighted—is touched. Daniel at first demurs. "Oh, God, please, no parties." But then he smiles and gives in.

⋙❧⋘

My husband says, "Oh, good. We haven't had one for a while."

I begin to call friends, to invite them.

I start with another favorite friend, Nora Y, a Berkeley novelist. (Thank God the Ys are not moving anywhere.) Nora, who also loves Judith, says terrific, a party, what a good idea.

And then she says, "But are they sure they'll like it there? I think I'd rather go to England, or southern France."

"Oh, so would I."

"Well, why don't we? Let's start an adult colony in the Dordogne, or somewhere like that."

"*Terrific.*"

We laugh and hang up.

❦❧

The next day I read in the paper that it has snowed in Jerusalem, where I had thought it also never snowed.

I go by to see Judith; she is busy—she says that it does sometimes snow in Jerusalem, but very rarely.

I report on the progress of the party.

❦❧

It is now raining steadily, the rain we needed.

❦❧

And for the first time in months almost anything seems possible.

Roses, Rhododendron

One dark and rainy Boston spring of many years ago, I spent all my after-school and evening hours in the living room of our antique-crammed Cedar Street flat, writing down what the Ouija board said to my mother. My father, a spoiled and rowdy Irishman, a sometime engineer, had run off to New Orleans with a girl, and my mother hoped to learn from the board if he would come back. Then, one night in May, during a crashing black thunderstorm (my mother was both afraid and much in awe of such storms), the board told her to move down South, to North Carolina, taking me and all the antiques she had been collecting for years, and to open a store in a small town down there. This is what we did, and shortly thereafter, for the first time in my life, I fell permanently in love: with a house, with a family of three people and with an area of countryside.

Perhaps too little attention is paid to the necessary preconditions of "falling in love"—I mean the state of mind or place that precedes one's first sight of the loved person (or house or land). In my own case, I remember the dark Boston afternoons as a precondition of love. Later on, for another important time, I recognized boredom in a job. And once the fear of growing old.

In the town that she had chosen, my mother, Margot (she picked out her own name, having been christened Margaret), rented a small house on a pleasant back street. It had a big surrounding screened-in porch, where she put most of the antiques, and she put a discreet sign out in the front yard: "Margot— Antiques." The store was open only in the afternoons. In the mornings and on Sundays, she drove around the countryside in our ancient and spacious Buick, searching for trophies among the area's country stores and farms and barns. (She is nothing if not enterprising; no one else down there had thought of doing that before.)

Although frequently embarrassed by her aggression—she thought nothing of making offers for furniture that was in use in a family's rooms—I often drove with her during those first few weeks. I was excited by the novelty of the landscape. The red clay banks that led up to the thick pine groves, the swollen brown creeks half hidden by flowering tangled vines. Bare, shaded yards from which rose gaunt, narrow houses. Chickens that scattered, barefoot children who stared at our approach.

"Hello, there. I'm Mrs. John Kilgore—Margot Kilgore—and I'm interested in buying old furniture. Family portraits. Silver."

Margot a big brassily bleached blonde in a pretty flowered silk dress and high-heeled patent sandals. A hoarse and friendly voice. Me a scrawny, pale, curious girl, about ten, in a blue linen dress with smocking across the bodice. (Margot has always had a passionate belief in good clothes, no matter what.)

On other days, Margot would say, "I'm going to look over my so-called books. Why don't you go for a walk or something, Jane?"

And I would walk along the sleepy, leafed-over streets, on the unpaved sidewalks, past houses that to me were as inviting and as interesting as unread books, and I would try to imagine what went on inside. The families. Their lives.

The main street, where the stores were, interested me least. Two-story brick buildings—dry-goods stores, with dentists' and lawyers' offices above. There was also a drugstore, with round marble tables and wire-backed chairs, at which wilting ladies sipped at their Cokes. (This was to become a favorite haunt of Margot's.) I preferred the civic monuments: a pre-Revolutionary Episcopal chapel of yellowish cracked plaster, and several tall white statues to the Civil War dead—all of them quickly overgrown with ivy or Virginia creeper.

These were the early nineteen-forties, and in the next few years the town was to change enormously. Its small textile factories would be given defense contracts (parachute silk); a Navy preflight school would be established at a neighboring university town. But at that moment it was a sleeping village. Untouched.

My walks were not a lonely occupation, but Margot worried that they were, and some curious reasoning led her to believe that a bicycle would help. (Of course, she turned out to be right.) We went to Sears, and she bought me a big new bike—blue, with balloon tires—on which I began to explore the outskirts of town and the countryside.

The house I fell in love with was about a mile out of town, on top of a hill. A small stone bank that was all overgrown with tangled roses led up to its yard, and pink and white roses climbed up a trellis to the roof of the front porch—the roof on which, later, Harriet and I used to sit and exchange our stores of erroneous sexual information. Harriet Farr was the daughter of the house. On one side of the house, there was what looked like a newer wing, with a bay window and a long side porch, below which the lawn sloped down to some flowering shrubs. There was a yellow rosebush, rhodo-dendron, a plum tree, and beyond were woods—pines, and oak and cedar trees. The effect was rich and careless, generous and somewhat mysterious. I was deeply stirred.

As I was observing all this, from my halted bike on the dusty white hilltop, a small, plump woman, very erect, came out of the front door and went over to a flower bed below the bay window. She sat down very stiffly. (Emily, who was Harriet's mother, had some terrible, never diagnosed trouble with her back; she generally wore a brace.) She was older than Margot, with very beautiful white hair that was badly cut in that butchered nineteen-thirties way.

From the first, I was fascinated by Emily's obvious dissimilarity to Margot. I think I was somehow drawn to her contradictions—the shapeless body held up with so much dignity, even while she was sitting in the dirt. The lovely chopped-off hair. (There were greater contradictions, which I learned of later—she was a Virginia Episcopalian who always voted for Norman Thomas, a feminist who always delayed meals for her tardy husband.)

Emily's hair was one of the first things about the Farr family that I mentioned to Margot after we became friends, Harriet and Emily and I, and I began to spend most of my time in that house.

"I don't think she's ever dyed it," I said, with almost conscious lack of tact.

Of course, Margot was defensive. "I wouldn't dye mine if I thought it would be a decent color on its own."

But by that time Margot's life was also improving. Business was fairly good, and she had finally heard from my father, who began to send sizable checks from New Orleans. He had found work with an oil company. She still asked the Ouija board if she would see him again, but her question was less obsessive.

The second time I rode past that house, there was a girl sitting on the front porch, reading a book. She was about my age. She looked up. The next time I saw her there, we both smiled. And the time after that (a Saturday morning in late June) she got up and slowly came out to the road, to where I had stopped, ostensibly to look at the view—the sweep of fields, the white highway, which wound down to the thick greenery bordering the creek, the fields and trees that rose in dim and distant hills.

"I've got a bike exactly like that," Harriet said indifferently, as though to deny the gesture of having come out to meet me.

For years, perhaps beginning then, I used to seek my opposite in friends. Inexorably following Margot, I was becoming a big blonde, with some of her same troubles. Harriet was cool and dark, with long gray eyes. A girl about to be beautiful.

"Do you want to come in? We've got some lemon cake that's pretty good."

Inside, the house was cluttered with odd mixtures of furniture. I glimpsed a living room, where there was a shabby sofa next to a pretty, "antique" table. We walked through a dining room that contained a decrepit mahogany table surrounded with delicate fruitwood chairs. (I had a horrifying moment of imagining Margot there, with her accurate eye—making offers in her harsh Yankee voice.) The walls were crowded with portraits and with nineteenth-century oils of bosky landscapes. Books overflowed from rows of shelves along the walls. I would have moved in at once.

We took our lemon cake back to the front porch and ate it there, overlooking that view. I can remember its taste vividly. It was light and tart and sweet, and a beautiful lemon color. With it, we drank cold milk, and then we had seconds and more milk, and we discussed what we liked to read.

We were both at an age to begin reading grown-up books, and there was some minor competition between us to see who had read more of them. Harriet won easily, partly because her mother reviewed books for the local paper, and had brought home Steinbeck, Thomas Wolfe, Virginia Woolf and Elizabeth Bowen. But we also found in common an enthusiasm for certain novels about English children. (Such snobbery!)

"It's the best cake I've ever had!" I told Harriet. I had already adopted something of Margot's emphatic style.

"It's very good," Harriet said judiciously. Then, quite casually, she added, "We could ride our bikes out to Laurel Hill."

We soared dangerously down the winding highway. At the bridge across the creek, we stopped and turned onto a narrow, rutted dirt road that followed the creek through woods as dense and as alien as a jungle would have been—thick pines with low sweeping branches, young leafed-out maples, peeling tall poplars, elms, brambles, green masses of honeysuckle. At times, the road was impassable, and we had to get off our bikes and push them along, over crevices and ruts, through mud or sand. And with all that we kept up our somewhat stilted discussion of literature.

"I love Virginia Woolf!"

"Yes, she's very good. Amazing metaphors."

I thought Harriet was an extraordinary person—more intelligent, more poised and prettier than any girl of my age I had ever known. I felt that she could become anything at all—a writer, an actress, a foreign correspondent (I went to a lot of movies). And I was not entirely wrong; she eventually became a some-times-published poet.

We came to a small beach, next to a place where the

creek widened and ran over some shallow rapids. On the other side, large gray rocks rose steeply. Among the stones grew isolated, twisted trees, and huge bushes with thick green leaves. The laurel of Laurel Hill. Rhododendron. Harriet and I took off our shoes and waded into the warmish water. The bottom squished under our feet, making us laugh, like the children we were, despite all our literary talk.

❦

Margot was also making friends. Unlike me, she seemed to seek her own likeness, and she found a sort of kinship with a woman named Dolly Murray, a rich widow from Memphis who shared many of Margot's superstitions—fear of thunderstorms, faith in the Ouija board. About ten years older than Margot, Dolly still dyed her hair red; she was a noisy, biased, generous woman. They drank gin and gossiped together, they met for Cokes at the drugstore and sometimes they drove to a neighboring town to have dinner in a restaurant (in those days, still a daring thing for unescorted ladies to do).

I am sure that the Farrs, outwardly a conventional family, saw me as a neglected child. I was so available for meals and overnight visits. But that is not how I experienced my life—I simply felt free. And an important thing to be said about Margot as a mother is that she never made me feel guilty for doing what I wanted to do. And of how many mothers can that be said?

There must have been a moment of "meeting" Emily, but I have forgotten it. I remember only her gentle presence, a soft voice and my own sense of love returned. Beautiful white hair, dark deep eyes and a wide mouth, whose corners turned and moved to express whatever she felt—amusement, interest, boredom, pain. I have never since seen such a vulnerable mouth.

I amused Emily; I almost always made her smile. She must have seen me as something foreign—a violent, enthusiastic Yankee. (I used forbidden words, like "God" and "damn.") Very unlike the decorous young Southern girl that she must have been, that Harriet almost was.

She talked to me a lot; Emily explained to me things about the South that otherwise I would not have picked up. "Virginians feel superior to everyone else, you know," she said, in her gentle (Virginian) voice. "Some people in my family were quite shocked when I married a man from North Carolina and came down here to live. And a Presbyterian at that! Of course, that's nowhere near as bad as a Baptist, but only Episcopalians really count." This was all said lightly, but I knew that some part of Emily agreed with the rest of her family.

❦

"How about Catholics?" I asked her, mainly to prolong the conversation. Harriet was at the dentist's, and Emily was sitting at her desk answering letters. I was perched on the sofa near her, and we both faced the sweeping green view. But since my father, Johnny Kilgore, was a lapsed Catholic, it was not an entirely frivolous question. Margot was a sort of Christian Scientist (her own sort).

"We hardly know any Catholics." Emily laughed, and then she sighed. "I do sometimes still miss Virginia. You know, when we drive up there I can actually feel the difference as we cross the state line. I've met a few people from South Carolina," she went on, "and I understand that people down there feel the same way Virginians do." (Clearly, she found this unreasonable.)

"West Virginia? Tennessee?"

"They don't seem Southern at all. Neither do Florida and Texas—not to me."

("Dolly says that Mrs. Farr is a terrible snob," Margot told me, inquiringly.

"In a way." I spoke with a new diffidence that I was trying to acquire from Harriet.

"Oh.")

Once, I told Emily what I had been wanting to say since my first sight of her. I said, "Your hair is so beautiful. Why don't you let it grow?"

She laughed, because she usually laughed at what I said, but at the same time she looked surprised, almost startled. I understood that what I had said was not improper but that she was totally unused to attentions of that sort from anyone, including herself. She didn't think about her hair. In a puzzled way, she said, "Perhaps I will."

Nor did Emily dress like a woman with much regard for herself. She wore practical, seersucker dresses and sensible, low shoes. Because her body had so little shape, no indentations (this must have been at least partly due to the back brace), I was surprised to notice that she had pretty, shapely legs. She wore little or no makeup on her sun- and wind-weathered face.

And what of Lawrence Farr, the North Carolina Presbyterian for whom Emily had left her people and her state? He was a small, precisely made man, with fine dark features. (Harriet looked very like him.) A lawyer, but widely read in literature, especially the English nineteenth century. He had a courtly manner, and sometimes a wicked tongue; melancholy eyes, and an odd, sudden, ratchety laugh. He looked ten years younger than Emily; the actual difference was less than two.

"Well," said Margot, settling into a Queen Anne chair—a new antique—on our porch one stifling hot July morning, "I heard some really interesting gossip about your friends."

Margot had met and admired Harriet, and Harriet liked her, too—Margot made Harriet laugh, and she praised Harriet's fine brown hair. But on some instinct (I am not sure whose) the parents had not met. Very likely, Emily, with her Southern social antennae, had somehow sensed that this meeting would be a mistake.

That morning, Harriet and I were going on a picnic in the woods to the steep rocky side of Laurel Hill, but I forced myself to listen, or half listen, to Margot's story.

"Well, it seems that some years ago Lawrence Farr fell absolutely madly in love with a beautiful young girl—in fact, the orphaned daughter of a friend of his. Terribly romantic. Of course, she loved him, too, but he felt so awful and guilty that they never did anything about it."

I did not like this story much; it made me obscurely uncomfortable, and I think that at some point both Margot and I wondered why she was telling it. Was she pointing out imperfections in my chosen other family? But I asked, in Harriet's indifferent voice, "He never kissed her?"

"Well, maybe. I don't know. But of course everyone in town knew all about it, including Emily Farr. And with her back! Poor woman," Margot added somewhat piously but with real feeling, too.

I forgot the story readily at the time. For one thing, there was something unreal about anyone as old as Lawrence Farr "falling in love." But looking back to Emily's face, Emily looking at Lawrence, I can see that pained watchfulness of a woman who has been hurt, and by a man who could always hurt her again.

In those days, what struck me most about the Farrs was their extreme courtesy to each other—something I had not seen before. Never a harsh word. (Of course, I did not know then about couples who cannot afford a single harsh word.)

❧

Possibly because of the element of danger (very slight—the slope was gentle), the roof over the front porch was one of the places Harriet and I liked to sit on warm summer nights when I was invited to stay over. There was a country silence, invaded at intervals by summer country sounds—the strangled croak of tree frogs from down in the glen; the crazy baying of a distant hound. There, in the heavy scent of roses, on the scratchy shingles, Harriet and I talked about sex.

"A girl I know told me that if you do it a lot your hips get very wide."

"My cousin Duncan says it makes boys strong if they do it."

"It hurts women a lot—especially at first. But I knew this girl from Santa Barbara, and she said that out there they say Filipinos can do it without hurting."

"Colored people do it a lot more than whites."

"Of course, they have all those babies. But in Boston so do Catholics!"

We are seized with hysteria. We laugh and laugh, so that Emily hears and calls up to us, "Girls, why haven't you-all gone to bed?" But her voice is warm and amused—she likes having us laughing up there.

And Emily liked my enthusiasm for lemon cake. She teased me about the amounts of it I could eat, and she continued to keep me supplied. She was not herself much of a cook—their maid, a young black girl named Evelyn, did most of the cooking.

Once, but only once, I saw the genteel and opaque

surface of that family shattered—saw those three people suddenly in violent opposition to each other, like shards of splintered glass. (But what I have forgotten is the cause—what brought about that terrible explosion?)

The four of us, as so often, were seated at lunch. Emily was at what seemed to be the head of the table. At her right hand was the small silver bell that summoned Evelyn to clear, or to bring a new course. Harriet and I across from each other, Lawrence across from Emily. (There was always a tentativeness about Lawrence's posture. He could have been an honored guest, or a spoiled and favorite child.) We were talking in an easy way. I have a vivid recollection only of words that began to career and gather momentum, to go out of control. Of voices raised. Then Harriet rushes from the room. Emily's face reddens dangerously, the corners of her mouth twitch downward and Lawrence, in an exquisitely icy voice, begins to lecture me on the virtues of reading Trollope. I am supposed to help him pretend that nothing has happened, but I can hardly hear what he is saying. I am in shock.

That sudden unleashing of violence, that exposed depth of terrible emotions might have suggested to me that the Farrs were not quite as I had imagined them, not the impeccable family in my mind—but it did not. I was simply and terribly—and selfishly—upset, and hugely relieved when it all seemed to have passed over.

❧

During that summer, the Ouija board spoke only gibberish to Margot, or it answered direct questions with repeated evasions:

"Will I ever see Johnny Kilgore again, in this life?"

"Yes no perhaps."

"Honey, that means you've got no further need of

the board, not right now. You've got to think every-thing out with your own heart and instincts," Dolly said.

Margot seemed to take her advice. She resolutely put the board away, and she wrote to Johnny that she wanted a divorce.

I had begun to notice that these days, on these sultry August nights, Margot and Dolly were frequently joined on their small excursions by a man named Larry—a jolly, redfaced man who was in real estate and who reminded me considerably of my father.

I said as much to Margot, and was surprised at her furious reaction. "They could not be more different, they are altogether opposite. Larry is a Southern gentleman. You just don't pay any attention to anyone but those Farrs."

A word about Margot's quite understandable jeal-ousy of the Farrs. Much later in my life, when I was unreasonably upset at the attachment of one of my own daughters to another family (unreasonable because her chosen group were all talented musicians, as she was), a wise friend told me that we all could use more than one set of parents—our relations with the original set are too intense, and need dissipating. But no one, certainly not silly Dolly, was around to comfort Margot with this wisdom.

The summer raced on. ("Not without dust and heat," Lawrence several times remarked, in his private ironic voice.) The roses wilted on the roof and on the banks next to the road. The creek dwindled, and beside it honeysuckle leaves lay limply on the vines. For weeks, there was no rain, and then, one afternoon, there came a dark torrential thunderstorm. Harriet and I sat on the side porch and watched its violent start—the black clouds seeming to rise from the horizon, the cracking, jagged streaks of lightning, the heavy, welcome rain.

And, later, the clean smell of leaves and grass and damp earth.

Knowing that Margot would be frightened, I thought of calling her, and then remembered that she would not talk on the phone during storms. And that night she told me, "The phone rang and rang, but I didn't think it was you, somehow."

"No."

"I had the craziest idea that it was Johnny. Be just like him to pick the middle of a storm for a phone call."

"There might not have been a storm in New Orleans."

But it turned out that Margot was right.

The next day, when I rode up to the Farrs' on my bike, Emily was sitting out in the grass where I had first seen her. I went and squatted beside her there. I thought she looked old and sad, and partly to cheer her I said, "You grow the most beautiful flowers I've ever seen."

She sighed, instead of smiling as she usually did. She said, "I seem to have turned into a gardener. When I was a girl, I imagined that I would grow up to be a writer, a novelist, and that I would have at least four children. Instead, I grow flowers and write book reviews."

I was not interested in children. "You never wrote a novel?"

She smiled unhappily. "No. I think I was afraid that I wouldn't come up to Trollope. I married rather young, you know."

And at that moment Lawrence came out of the house, immaculate in white flannels.

He greeted me, and said to Emily, "My dear, I find that I have some rather late appointments, in Hillsboro. You won't wait dinner if I'm a trifle late?"

(Of course she would; she always did.)

"No. Have a good time," she said, and she gave him the anxious look that I had come to recognize as the way she looked at Lawrence.

❦

Soon after that, a lot happened very fast. Margot wrote to Johnny (again) that she wanted a divorce, that she intended to marry Larry. (I wonder if this was ever true.) Johnny telephoned—not once but several times. He told her that she was crazy, that he had a great job with some shipbuilders near San Francisco—a defense contract. He would come to get us, and we would all move out there. Margot agreed. We would make a new life. (Of course, we never knew what happened to the girl.)

I was not as sad about leaving the Farrs and that house, that town, those woods as I was to be later, looking back. I was excited about San Francisco, and I vaguely imagined that someday I would come back and that we would all see each other again. Like parting lovers, Harriet and I promised to write each other every day.

And for quite a while we did write several times a week. I wrote about San Francisco—how beautiful it was: the hills and pastel houses, the sea. How I wished that she could see it. She wrote about school and friends. She described solitary bike rides to places we had been. She told me what she was reading.

In high school, our correspondence became more generalized. Responding perhaps to the adolescent mores of the early nineteen-forties, we wrote about boys and parties; we even competed in making ourselves sound "popular." The truth (my truth) was that I was sometimes popular, often not. I had, in fact, a stormy adolescence. And at that time I developed what was to be a long-lasting habit. As I reviewed a situation in which I had been ill-advised or impulsive, I would re-enact the whole scene in my mind with Harriet in my own role—Harriet, cool and controlled, more intelligent, prettier. Even more than I wanted to see her again, I wanted to *be* Harriet.

Johnny and Margot fought a lot and stayed together, and gradually a sort of comradeship developed between them in our small house on Russian Hill.

I went to Stanford, where I half-heartedly studied history. Harriet was at Radcliffe, studying American literature, writing poetry.

We lost touch with each other.

Margot, however, kept up with her old friend Dolly, by means of Christmas cards and Easter notes, and Margot thus heard a remarkable piece of news about Emily Farr. Emily "up and left Lawrence without so much as a by-your-leave," said Dolly, and went to Washington, D.C., to work in the Folger Library. This news made me smile all day. I was so proud of Emily. And I imagined that Lawrence would amuse himself, that they would both be happier apart.

By accident, I married well—that is to say, a man whom I still like and enjoy. Four daughters came at uncalculated intervals, and each is remarkably unlike her sisters. I named one Harriet, although she seems to have my untidy character.

From time to time, over the years, I would see a poem by Harriet Farr, and I always thought it was marvelous, and I meant to write her. But I distrusted my reaction. I had been (I was) so deeply fond of Harriet (Emily, Lawrence, that house and land) and besides, what would I say—"I think your poem is marvelous"? (I have since learned that this is neither an inadequate nor an unwelcome thing to say to writers.) Of course, the true reason for not writing was that there was too much to say.

Dolly wrote to Margot that Lawrence was drinking

"all over the place." He was not happier without Emily. Harriet, Dolly said, was traveling a lot. She married several times and had no children. Lawrence developed emphysema, and was in such bad shape that Emily quit her job and came back to take care of him—whether because of feelings of guilt or duty or possibly affection, I didn't know. He died, lingeringly and miserably, and Emily, too, died, a few years later—at least partly from exhaustion, I would imagine.

❧

Then, at last, I did write Harriet, in care of the magazine in which I had last seen a poem of hers. I wrote a clumsy, gusty letter, much too long, about shared pasts, landscapes, the creek. All that. And as soon as I had mailed it I began mentally rewriting, seeking more elegant prose.

When for a long time I didn't hear from Harriet, I felt worse and worse, cumbersome, misplaced—as too often in life I had felt before. It did not occur to me that an infrequently staffed magazine could be at fault.

Months later, her letter came—from Rome, where she was then living. Alone, I gathered. She said that she was writing it at the moment of receiving mine. It was a long, emotional and very moving letter, out of character for the Harriet that I remembered (or had invented).

She said, in part: "It was really strange, all that time when Lawrence was dying, and God! so long! and as though 'dying' were all that he was doing—Emily, too, although we didn't know that—all that time the picture that moved me most, in my mind, that moved me to tears, was not of Lawrence and Emily but of you and me. On our bikes at the top of the hill outside our house. Going somewhere. And I first thought that that picture simply symbolized something irretrievable, the

218

lost and irrecoverable past, as Lawrence and Emily would be lost. And I'm sure that was partly it.

"But they were so extremely fond of you—in fact, you were a rare area of agreement. They missed you, and they talked about you for years. It's a wonder that I wasn't jealous, and I think I wasn't only because I felt included in their affection for you. They liked me best with you.

"Another way to say this would be to say that we were all three a little less crazy and isolated with you around, and, God knows, happier."

An amazing letter, I thought. It was enough to make me take a long look at my whole life, and to find some new colors there.

❧

A postscript: I showed Harriet's letter to my husband, and he said, "How odd. She sounds so much like you."

What Should I Have Done?

A couple of weeks ago I had an experience so upsetting that my breath tightens, my heart beats too fast, crazily, whenever I think of it, and I do think of it, obsessively. I wonder what I should have done.

The incident that so upset me was really the final chapter in a rather long story, the story of my friendship with Maggie, and looking at the whole of it, I wonder if all along I could not have acted differently—although it is hard to see how I could have saved her life.

This last chapter, then, took place at a large dinner party. It began when a certain man came in and sat across the room from me, and I was filled with such pure rage at him that I trembled, my blood ran cold and I longed to get up and cross the room, to slap his face very hard and to say something violent, possibly obscene. Instead, I suppose to explain what must have been a visible reaction, I told the woman on my left an abbreviated version of the cause of my fury. The man sat there on the other side of the room, smiling, plump and red-faced, white-haired, a happy priest, out in good company.

A couple of relevant facts about myself: I am a

lapsed Episcopalian, not a virulent anti-Catholic. Generally nonviolent, a "liberal" (actually I am a closet radical). No more ill-tempered, really, than the next person. You know the type.

We were in a large room; the dinner was buffet. The priest could not have heard the story I was telling, but he could have figured it out, not being at all stupid—reading a great deal from my expression. In any case he left the party very early, before I had said or done anything directly to him. And so I still don't know.

⌘

The real story begins a long time ago, in the Forties, during what was called Freshman Orientation Week, in a good New England college. I am in the smoking room, and across the room I see a red-haired (in pin curls) dark-eyed girl in pale-green cotton pajamas, who is saying, in a rather tight, shy voice, "I'm supposed to have an aptitude in history." I thought, Well, how terrific for you.

But on another level I had heard her say, *They* have invented something called an "aptitude in history," and stuck it on me; what idiots they are.

⌘

In any case, Maggie, as we will call her here, and I, over the next weeks and months and years, became the closest friends.

Maggie: an exceptionally bright, complex, distrusting, witty girl, an Irish Catholic, from Philadelphia. At that time she wanted to be an engineer, which is what her father was. ("I want to build *bridges*." Such an exotic ambition was perhaps too much for her, and she soon gave it up.) She was not pretty, by those exacting Forties standards. Beautiful rich red hair, which she

221

tended either to curl too tightly or to neglect entirely. Small brown eyes (she sometimes referred to herself as Rat Eyes), tiny breasts and a tendency to wide hips. Not generally "popular" with boys, but a girl of strong sexual feelings (this is important to the story). Too often, when she did have a date, she would drink too much, nervously, and then "neck heavily" with the boy—always, unfortunately, with the sort of boy who would conclude from such behavior that she was not "nice," and would not call her again.

We were friends mainly on the basis of shared or similar humor: we made each other laugh for hours, sitting in the smoking room or out on the drafty steps of our dormitory. We made elaborate fantasies together. I remember one involving Cassandra—"For God's sake don't invite her, she's so gloomy." Another about a mythical family named White, who subscribed to the *National Geographic* and had linoleum on their bedroom floor. Several routines involving what we thought were funny accents: Brooklynese, East Boston.

During one vacation, Maggie came to visit me at home, and I introduced her to all the friends of my childhood, those nice Southern girls and boys; I am from Washington, D.C.

We had a wonderful time laughing at them, imitating, late at night, after parties. The boys took her out on dates, and she had the brief experience of a popular visiting girl, though of course they thought her "fast" and didn't write, as otherwise they might have, inviting her to V.M.I. or Charlottesville.

And I went to Philadelphia to stay with Maggie and her parents. Her mother was small and round, voluble and affectionate; her father, whom Maggie resembled, was silent, almost dour, but one sensed in him a striking and original intelligence, and wit.

❧❦❧

During her senior year, a rich Midwestern boy named Bill fell in love with Maggie, and there ensued a frantic courtship: flowers and presents, much eating and drinking and dancing in expensive places (Maggie was somewhat greedy in that way), a lot of rushing around the New England countryside in Bill's red convertible.

As the Best Friend, I was introduced to Bill, and I didn't like him very much at first. He was O.K., but so ordinary, and Maggie was remarkable; no one else was so funny or *so bright*. But then as Bill's mania for her continued, along with the orchids and jewelry, the steak and lobster dinners, dancing on the Ritz roof, I thought that he must be at least all right, and Maggie was in love with him. She said so, one night, quite out of character: we didn't generally talk about strong feelings—or, rather, she didn't; I'm afraid I always have. They were going to get married.

Bill wanted them to marry right away, or at the latest the following fall, when we would all be out of college. Maggie, for whatever reasons of her own (unspoken and perhaps unconscious), wanted to postpone it. I was enlisted by Bill to plead his cause, a mission that romantically appealed to me, but I soon saw the uselessness of what I was saying. Irrefutably Maggie said, "Why rush?"

And so we all graduated and Bill went back to his Midwestern city to start work for his father, in whatever they did, making a lot of money; and still there were no definite wedding plans. Maggie was holding off.

And then it was all over, Bill not writing and Maggie scrupulously sending back (postpaid, insured) his expensive presents.

I don't know quite what happened, nor, I think, did she. And, remember, we didn't actually talk a lot, Maggie and I; we just made our jokes. Once, somewhat later, she said, of Bill and his defection, "I think it was

223

a combination of parental pressure—I wasn't just what they had in mind—and, given him, most likely another girl." Much later still, she said of Bill, "He really wasn't very nice."

At another time, during an uncharacteristically intimate conversation about sex, she said, "Bill and I never actually went all the way, but everything but."

❦

Now we skip several years, during which I got married and Maggie, as my maid of honor, comforted my bridegroom in the face of my curious ambivalent behavior. "*Maggie* was always around to hold my hand," he accusingly said. (I knew the marriage was wrong, but while it was taking place I could not admit such a gross mistake. An unhappily familiar story.)

My husband and I moved out West, and after a few years (for professional reasons: she had become an economist, not an engineer) Maggie came out too, with a good teaching job, and we were friends again.

Once she invited us to dinner, and there was a young man with whom she was obviously "involved"—a dullish person, I thought; and then a few weeks later she said that it was all off. I doubt if it was ever serious (meaning, I doubt if they went to bed).

And then I became aware that she was tremendously involved with someone; he came for dinner often and presumably stayed on. I am not sure how I knew this; certainly Maggie did not say it. Someone whom I was not to meet. Married—a sick wife? I was on the whole pleased; he seemed lavish with champagne and roses, and as I have said Maggie liked that kind of thing, and she looked happy, and loved. But in another sense I was not pleased; I would have wanted a more complete relationship for her, of course. By that time I knew a little about the disadvantages of the illicit myself.

And then—and then she told me that she was pregnant. Of course (as a free-thinking Protestant) I counseled an abortion. Interestingly, so did her mother. I insisted that that was her only solution, if she couldn't get married. (We are now talking about the Fifties, when women from San Francisco went to Seattle or Mexico for abortions.) But she pointed out that no, as a Catholic she could not have an abortion. (I have not said this: her religion was another thing we never discussed; it was simply there, a fact of her life.) She was going down to some nuns near Los Angeles, who took in unmarried mothers, who arranged for placements. *Placements*.

"Is your friend being nice about it?" I asked her that.

"Oh, *very*," she said with some warmth.

Pregnant, Maggie looked pale and fat and wholly miserable. Her skin broke out and her small eyes seemed to recede.

She gave birth to a red-haired daughter.

And the baby was placed.

❧❧❧

Maggie stayed pale and fat. Not curled hair (sometimes not washed). Sad old clothes, despite her good job.

❧❧❧

Skip more years. I was divorced and involved with a man who was married, and I thought I was pregnant. I went to Maggie's for dinner, and we discussed symptoms.

I drank too much wine and in a somewhat maudlin mood I asked her if she still saw her friend.

"Oh, yes, all the time." Not saying, We still love each other tremendously. But that was clear. And I looked across at Maggie, in her old sweater, her hair dull and lank (at that time I was making the most excruciating efforts as to frosted, shining hair, and terrific clothes—all for that man), and I thought, How wonderful not to have to make such an effort, to be so secure in someone's love.

And so I said, "Oh, Maggie, can't you live together or something? Anyone can get a divorce these days."

"Uh—you haven't guessed what's wrong?" A very tight voice.

I muttered about a sick wife, maybe crazy—

As Maggie is saying, "He's a priest."

My mind literally reeled with shock, revolving in images of long black skirts, and I asked the only thing that came to mind as possible to ask: "Jesus—what do you call him?"

She smiled, and in her wry, shy voice ("I'm supposed to have an aptitude in history") she said, "Sometimes Father Feeny. Sometimes Dick."

❦

So, a few years later, at a party I am introduced to a handsome priest, whose name I miss. He, however, has heard a mention of the college I went to (how did that come up? I can't remember) and he says, "Ah, yes, I know a girl who went there. Did you by chance know Maggie————?"

"Yes, very well." (My breath is suddenly tight.) "I'm sorry, I didn't catch your name."

"Father Feeny. Richard Feeny." And he beams.

I have had two strong drinks. I am not drunk, but not wholly controlled, and very upset.

Then, quite incredibly (to me), he says, "Well, since you're a friend of Maggie's, I can tell you that I'm rather worried about her. She looks bad, and lonely. You look like the sort of young woman who knows a lot of people, perhaps you could introduce her to someone. She really should marry."

I am wild-eyed, stammering.

Insensitive (perhaps he has also had a couple of drinks), he continues, "Lately she's been talking about a former fiancé. Bill? It's sad, as though she wants to say that she could have married."

I want to say, You are horrible—you hypocrite! I hate you! But to say that or anything like it would be to betray Maggie, her confidence in me. You see? He had me, utterly. I got away from him as soon as I could.

❦

Over the phone a couple of days later I say to Maggie: "It was really strange, meeting him, and of course his not knowing I knew who he was. And then his wishing you would marry—"

In a tight, judicious voice she says, "Well, I guess at least partly he does wish that."

❦

After that some terrible drift apart began, and at last Maggie and I were not seeing each other. Our lives diverged, and I think that she also regretted telling me so much; we all know how that works.

❦

And then a few years ago I read in our college magazine that Maggie had died, of cancer. Grief—rage—anguish: I felt all that, and some guilt at never having called her, instead of, from time to time, thinking that I would.

And I wondered, Just when did that start, that malevolent process of her cells?

Which brings us to a couple of weeks ago, when I again saw the priest. Saw Father Feeny—Richard, Dick.

And wanted to hit him, or to say, Well, your daughter must be almost twenty by now, wouldn't you say? Or, Have you been saying a lot of masses for Maggie? Do you think they help?

Well, as I have said, he left before I could do or say anything, except to stare at him with a pure electric hatred—he must have felt it.

And now I wonder if my feelings were not somewhat unfair. He fell in love with Maggie and took her to bed (she felt very loved by him, I am sure of that). He was no more sexually restrained than the rest of us are, although he was supposed to have been. In his way he was kind and generous to her. Probably it is too much for me to have expected heroism of him, which in my view would have been to leave the priesthood and marry Maggie, although I do think he should have. (It is also possible that Maggie didn't want him to do this, for her own good Catholic reasons.)

But I still wonder what, if anything, I should have done, or said.

For Good

~~~~~~

"How I hate California! God, no one will ever know how much I hate it here," cries out Pauline Field, a once-famous abstract-expressionist painter. It is lunchtime on a ferociously cold Sunday late in June—in a beach house near San Francisco: Pauline's house—and her lunch party that is assembled there in her enclosed patio, drinking sangrias. Almost no one (in fact only one person) pays any attention to Pauline, who tends to speak in an exaggerated way. She is a huge strong woman, dressed outrageously in pink; she has wild white hair and consuming dark-brown eyes. It is possible that she has made this impassioned complaint before.

The house is some three or four years old; those years (the years, incidentally, of Pauline's most recent marriage) and the relentless wind have almost silvered the shingled walls, and beach grass has grown up through the slats of the planked-over patio, where now all those guests, twenty or so, are standing with their cold fruity drinks, their backs to the wind and to the sea. The drive home, over steep winding hills and beside great wooded canyons, will be somewhat dangerous even for a sober driver; these weak drinks are the inspiration of Pauline's (third) husband, Stephen, a cautious former alcoholic.

The one person who paid attention to Pauline is also the only person who is looking out to the churning gray sea: a young girl, about twelve, Nell Ashbury, from New York; she is visiting her father and her stepmother. She listened to Pauline because her hostess has come across to her more vividly than any of the other adults present (discounting her father, Jason Ashbury, the writer, about whom she has the most passionate curiosity, not knowing him well at all). Pauline, to Nell, is more *present* than anyone else there. Her mother's Village circle includes a lot of writers, editors, agents; Nell is tired of literary people, who all talk too much. Perhaps she herself will be a painter, like Pauline? And Pauline listens; so many grown-ups (her mother's writers) ask questions and then don't wait to hear the answer. Pauline is kind; she has in fact wrapped reed-thin Nell in an old Irish sweater of her own, in which the girl now sits, enveloped—it comes down to her knees—looking out across a grass-tufted rise of sand to the turbulent sea, and thinking, Pacific?

But at Pauline's words—"I hate California"—Nell has turned to listen, and it occurs to her that she does not like it here much either; it is terribly windy and cold, not at all like a summer day at a real beach, not like Crane's Beach, at Ipswich, where she and her mother go for the month of August every summer. Nell has a tendency to take people at their word (she believes that Pauline hates California), and partly because she is so young, she believes that what is said is meant, for good.

Nell also (half-consciously) understands Pauline to mean that she does not like her party, her guests—and possibly does not like her husband, the blond man, rather short, who is pouring out the reddish drinks.

"It's not a place that's fit for human beings,"

declaims Pauline, who has not had a show of her paintings for years, although she still works, if spasmodically, and who has unhappily become used to inattention. "Perhaps mountain lions," she continues. "Feel that wind, in *June*."

Pauline's size is a further reason for Nell's instinct about her not liking her husband. "Women who hate their husbands always put on weight," Nell's mother has said, herself purposefully thin (and unremarried), and Nell has as yet found no evidence against this theory. Her stepmother, who visibly "adores" her father, is even trimmer than Nell's mother is. Given the ten years or so difference in their ages, they look rather alike, Nell thinks—and would of course not say to either of them. Brown-skinned blondes, blue-eyed, rather athletic. What her father likes?

In fact Nell has seen rather few fat women among the friends of either parent, and this too gives Pauline a certain interest: what *nerve*, to be so large. And her size is somehow sexy, all that energetic flesh. The other guests look vaguely alike and are dressed quite similarly: they are in stylishly good shape; they wear pants and expensive old sweaters.

Nell herself is physically a curious replica of her father: sandy-haired, with light-gray eyes. Everyone has remarked on the likeness, and Nell has sometimes wondered if this is one thing that makes him uneasy with her: it must be strange for Jason to see his coloring, his own long nose and impossibly high brow on a girl, a thin young girl. Sometimes Nell catches him staring at her in an unnerved way, and he seems not to know what to say to her. The phrase "pale imitation" has unfortunately stuck in her mind. They were divorced so long ago, Jason and her mother, when Nell was a baby and Jason a hugely successful novelist. On the heels of his greatest success—that rarity, a book that six or eight superior critics praised and that several hundred thousand people bought—he stopped writing entirely. He has lived a lot in Italy, in southern France and Greece.

❦

Although she is the one complaining about the weather, Pauline has not dressed to defend herself from it: the longsleeved pink cotton smock from which her spatulate-fingered, muscular brown hands extend is thin ("Fat women always love bright colors," Nell's mother has said, safe in navy or black); she is barefoot, and sand adheres to her large brown feet. She says, "I can't bear this wind!"

"Well, Pauline," says Jason, in his glancing, non-serious way that no one seems to know how to take (*is* he serious?), "you could chuck it all and run off to some warmer clime."

So, Nell thinks, he too has been listening to Pauline?

Pauline's great eyes flash across him; she says, "I just may."

But her husband, blond Stephen, has spoken much more loudly than she. "Pauline would rather stick around and make dramatic complaints," he says, sounding smug with his knowledge (and possession?) of Pauline.

Obviously these two men, Nell's father and Stephen, do not like each other much, and Nell begins to regard the party with slightly more interest. Just possibly something could happen? In general, her parents' friends do not make scenes, just talk, and she had sometimes thought that it would be more fun if they did.

"In fact I might join you there, wherever," Jason continues, as though Stephen had not spoken. "It is awfully goddam cold." He turns to his small blond wife. "And how would you like that, my love?"

Neither what he said nor his look has been clear: did he mean that he would take his wife or leave her there in the California cold? Nell's stepmother visibly does not know, but in a calm, controlled way she says, "Well, in the meantime I think I'll go inside. It *is* terribly cold." She starts in, and everyone begins to follow her, as though an excuse or perhaps a leader was needed.

Jason laughs, as Nell wonders why: At what private joke?

"I need help!" wildly says Pauline as people are trooping past her into the house, and then, in a more rational way, she addresses Nell—who has taken her seriously and is staring in dismay. "Nell, do come in the kitchen with me. You look as though you were good at sorting things out."

The kitchen is farther away and thus more separate from the living room than is usual in the houses Nell has known. She and Pauline walk down a hall, past bedrooms, to what is the largest room in the house: a huge square, two stories high, with a backward-looking view of steep, ravined hills, all shades and shapes and varieties of green, here and there patched with sunlight, in other areas cloud-darkened, almost black. "There's only one painter out here who can do that," says Pauline (sadly? enviously? Nell can't tell). "I've never tried. Perhaps I should? This is my favorite room," she says. "I like to be alone here. I can't bear people who come out to try to help me—I can't be helped." She laughs, a short harsh definite sound. "Of course I don't mean you, little Nell—I asked you in." And Nell is then given a large handful of silver which, for a moment, she is afraid that she is supposed to polish; this has not been done for some time.

"Just sort it out into little piles," instructs Pauline. "You know, to be wrapped in a napkin. Something for everyone. And now tell me all about your mother."

"She's fine," Nell automatically says, and then asks, "Did you know her?"

"Oh, yes," says Pauline, sounding bored. "We all used to know each other. But that was terribly long ago. In the Forties, in fact. Of course we were terribly young."

The *Forties*. Wanting to know more (what was everyone like then? what was her father like?), Nell has understood that Pauline does not want to answer questions—she will talk more or less to herself.

Pauline is drinking vodka from a wineglass. "God, how I hate sangria," she abruptly says, in much her tone of hating California. And then she asks, "Are you very tired of conversations about why your father doesn't write anymore?"

Nell hesitates, at a loss. "No, we don't talk about that much," she honestly says, at last.

"Oh, I suppose not. Your mother would have lost interest, lucky for her. Out here it's quite a favorite topic, among his friends. That's partly what I mean about California. It's as vacuous as it is windy, in fact it's a chilly windbag of a place." And she laughs, in a pleased way—she will clearly say this again. "The truth is," she then continues, "Jason is scared. His last book was so good that it scared him to death, almost."

Nell smiles politely. She is the sort of child to whom adults often talk, perhaps in some (erroneous) belief that innocence prevents her understanding. She is by now used to nearly incomprehensible remarks that later make considerable sense, and so now she tucks away this notion of California, and of her father's work. And she wonders: Is Pauline talking about herself?

The salad that Pauline is making, in a huge wooden bowl on the large butcher-block table, also looks (at first) familiar to Nell: several kinds of lettuce, thinly sliced onion, parsley. But then other things from dishes in the giant refrigerator are added: fish-smelling things, pink, and indistinguishable in shape. "Mussels and clams," Pauline says. "*Fruits de mer.* They'll absolutely hate it. Everyone except your father. He loves all this stuff too."

Did Pauline once love her father? Did they have an affair, back in the Forties? This thought, or question, has been slowly forming in Nell's mind. Nell's mother and her friends talk a lot about people having affairs, which Nell takes to mean making out with someone you're not married to. She is very interested, although she herself has so far only observed other kids at parties smoking grass, making out.

And she of course enjoys being talked to by adults, but only up to a point. She does not like it—is in fact frightened—when voices begin to slur, when eyes grow vague and at the same time wild. She now with alarm observes the onset of these symptoms in Pauline, as Pauline says, staring at Nell too intently, "If I could only get thin again, then I could work. It's all this fat that holds me."

Nell can no more imagine being fat than she can being dead, and she has only the vaguest ideas about work. But she has, still, a strong sense that Pauline even semi-drunk is someone to whom she should pay attention.

Pauline says, "The really important thing is never to marry."

Well, Nell had decided that for herself already, years ago.

Just then a dark man whom Nell has not much noticed before comes into the room, and Pauline embraces him in a way that Nell has seen before: grown-ups in a kitchen (usually) lurching at each other.

Pauline croons, "Ah, my long-lost love, why couldn't everything last?"

There are tears in her manic eyes that to Nell look real, but the man seems not to take them seriously. He pats her shoulder in a dismissing way; he even says, "*There,*" and he goes back out, looking embarrassed.

Pauline gives Nell a sober, calculating look of complicity; was she then pretending with that man to be drunk, or much drunker than she is, in order to make fun of him? What will she do next? Nell fully believes in Pauline's desperation.

Now Pauline goes over to the oven, and efficiently (undrunkenly) with asbestos gloves she removes a huge steaming garlic-smelling casserole. This and the salad and the napkin-wrapped silver are placed on a wire-wheeled cart, and propelled into the living room. Nell follows at a little distance in her wake.

People line up and help themselves. Not sure what to do, or where to be, Nell is surprised to see her father coming toward her, carrying two full plates, saying, "Come on, let's go over there."

And then, when they are seated, in a tone unusual for him, with her, he says, "I hope this isn't too bad a party for you? I didn't know there'd be so many people. And somehow I wanted you to meet Pauline. Anyway, sometimes it's easier to talk in the middle of a crowd, have you noticed that yet? And we haven't had much of a chance to talk, have we? Have I seemed preoccupied? The thing is—please, you won't mention this to anyone? I'm sure you won't. I wanted to tell you—"

Nell is to find that life often provides too much at once: just as her heart jumps with pleasure at her father's telling her something important, in confidence—just at that crucial moment they both hear Pauline shouting from across the room; they see Pauline wildly waving her arms—Pauline making a scene. "Well, goodbye, one and all. I'm off for a walk. Don't eat and run—I'll be gone for hours. Unless—would anyone like to come along?" There is a terrible pause, especially terrible for Nell, who believes that the

236

invitation, or summons, was for her—who is frozen in her corner. "Well, then, O.K. Sorry I asked." A door is slammed, and Pauline is gone.

Nell looks at her father, and she sees her own feelings apparent on his face, written across his features so similar to her own: Jason looks stricken, deeply shocked, as she is. And Nell is aware of real panic: a friend of her mother's, a woman writer who often drank too much, committed suicide at last. What will happen to Pauline? Will she plunge drunkenly into that cold bleak ocean, that terrible Pacific?

She looks questioningly at her father, who only says, *"Well,"* in an exhausted way.

Unable not to, Nell asks him, "You wanted to tell me—"

He looks at her forgetfully. "Oh, just a novel. I've begun one."

Naturally enough, people do eat and run. In a flustered way Stephen serves coffee, which everyone seems to gulp, and then there is a general movement toward cars.

❦

The drive home, to Nell, does not seem dangerous; she trusts her father's skill at the wheel. And the scenery is extraordinary: once they have left the beach, and the now golden glimpses of the sea, they climb steeply into what could be a rain forest, dense variegated vegetation, trees, giant ferns—into what must have been the view from Pauline's kitchen, and Nell remembers what Pauline said about its being a country for mountain lions. It smells of bay leaves.

Her stepmother is talking about Pauline. "Well, I never saw drink hit her quite like that. She has put on weight, hasn't she? Anyway, she always manages to put out a great lunch. Although I could have done without all those bits of seafood in the salad. I wonder why she ever married Stephen. She seems to fall in love with giants and marry pygmies. What do you suppose struck her, finally? Three ex-lovers all suddenly at the same party?"

Nell finds all this vaguely disturbing, less vaguely unpleasant. She is still worried about Pauline; why is no one else worried?

Her father makes a sound that for him is completely in character, that is brief and impossible to read. And Nell is suddenly aware of a rush of the most intense and private love for him.

✦❈✦

A month or so later Nell and her mother are sitting on the beach—Crane's Beach, at Ipswich. A perfect beach, of fine white silk sand that squeaks underfoot. Dunes, grass. And a perfect hot still day. From time to time Nell has been thinking of Pauline. (She has gathered that nothing horrible happened to her; someone would have said.) Now she wonders if this was the way Pauline thought a beach should be, and that summers should produce this sort of day? Yes, probably, she decides, and then she experiences again a tiny pang of guilt-regret at not having gone for that walk with Pauline, Pauline leaving her own party, so furiously. Although, of course, it was impossible at the time; she was talking to her father.

These days Nell's mother is extremely happy, almost giddily so: a man she knows, in fact an old family friend, is getting a divorce, and he and Nell's mother are going to get married. He works for a firm that is moving to Houston, and that is where they will all live. Houston, Texas. "We can take wonderful trips to Mexico, and New Orleans," her mother has said, with her new young laugh. Nell wonders about parties in Houston, and what will happen to her there.

The sea is very calm today; the barest waves, translucent, lap the sand, where at the edge, on their crazy useless-looking legs, the sandpipers skitter past. And overhead white gulls wheel and dip, as though drunk with sunlight. Pauline would love it here, is what at that moment Nell thinks. She is also thinking that there are only about four more months until Christmas, which is when she can go to visit her father again. It has been agreed that she can now go more often.

Her mother, reading letters beside Nell on the sand, suddenly laughs. Nell has seen that this one is from her father, whose letters to his former wife do not usually make her laugh. "Well," her mother says, "everyone seems to be breaking up these days." (Does she mean Nell's father? Will she have a new stepmother? This quick notion is enough to make Nell queasy for an instant as her mother reads on.) "You met Pauline Field, didn't you, darling? Well, she's up and left poor old Stephen, and she's gone off to San Miguel de Allende, to study painting there."

Nell makes an ambiguous noise, not unlike her father's noncommittal sound. Then she asks, "That's probably good for her to do, isn't it?"

"I suppose. She was quite terrific, in her way." Nell's mother adds, "I never understood that marriage to Stephen. Or any of her marriages, for that matter."

Nell says what she has not said before: "She was sort of upset at her party that we went to. *She* said"—they both know that this *"she"* refers to Nell's stepmother— "something about three ex-lovers at the same party. Can a husband be counted as an ex-lover?"

Her mother laughs a lot. "Darling, what a marvelous question. Well, actually one of them would of course have been Jason. They had a tremendous love affair, just before me. Sometimes I thought he'd never get over it, and I used to wish he'd married her. Instead of me. Maybe he would have gone on writing, or at least got her out of his system."

Digesting this news, which is not news at all, but something deeply known or felt before, Nell experiences a kind of gladness. Things seem to fit, or to have sorted themselves out, after all.

And, later still, although she has been told that San Miguel is in the middle of Mexico, nowhere near the coast, and although she has not been told that her father and stepmother are separating, what she imagines is—Jason and Pauline (a Pauline brown and thin, renewed) on a bright hot windless tropical beach. For good.